FALLEN ANGEL
BROKEN SAINT DUET PART TWO

E.M. GAYLE

GYPSY INK BOOKS

Copyright © 2021 by Eliza Gayle

Writing as E.M. Gayle

https://emgayle.com/newsletter

All rights reserved.

No part of this book may be reproduced in any form or by any electronic or mechanical means, including information storage and retrieval systems, without written permission from the author, except for the use of brief quotations in a book review.

CHAPTER 1

Ronin

Well, hell. That had not gone exactly as planned. Although it had been more than a little entertaining. I crossed the room of my own opulent suite at The Sinclair and proceeded to pour a double scotch. After the day I'd had, I needed it. Watching Nova lose her shit and throw the pouch of diamonds in the Fed's face had been the highlight of the confrontation. Even if it made for bad timing.

It might have caused a wrinkle in my plans, but I was confident I could work through any issues it might cause. Rock Reed was an annoying thorn in my side, and I needed him out of the game. Toying with a Boy Scout like him always came with challenges and upped the stakes. A scenario I didn't usually mind.

The higher the stakes, the better the payoff when I finally won. And I would win this game. Long before anyone else even realized they were playing.

Besides, it had been time for Nova to learn that her lover was a federal agent. There was toying with the Feds, and then there was being stupid. She'd teetered on that edge for quite some time, and like it or not, it had to stop.

I'd also grown tired of watching them fuck. That asshole didn't deserve a banshee in the sack like her. If she needed a man to submit to, I was more than happy to offer myself as tribute.

The diamonds, however, complicated things.

I reached into my pocket, pulled out a tiny Ziploc bag, and tossed it onto the table. The gems inside sparkled in the spotlight of the small lamp. Normally, they wouldn't matter, but in this case they did. Anything and everything Anthony Cullotta wanted, I planned to take away. Before I completed my mission here, I intended to watch him squirm. And then beg. A smile crossed my face as I brought the glass back to my lips.

They always begged.

The moment they realized nothing they said or did would stop their imminent death, they gave in and begged for life.

Nova had no idea how close she'd come to catching me when I swapped these for fakes. My brilliant little fiancée had a lot going for her, but seeing what was right in front of her wasn't one of them. *Fiancée*. I'd begun to consider that word in unexpected ways. A part of me still thought it might be fun to go through with it, just to see where it took the game next.

Marry the girl. Fuck the girl. Then make the girl watch me kill her father.

Hell, after today, she might enjoy it. That bastard had an evil heart. He had no love for his own daughter, or likely anyone else. Or loyalty. Love might not be important, but loyalty...it was everything.

Sadly, the minute Reed found out the pouch of diamonds in his possession were fakes, he'd be back at her doorstep like a bad penny. I never really understood that expression, but my father loved it. In my opinion, bad penny was never a strong enough description for someone who had become a pain in my ass.

I could kill him.

A bullet between his eyes sounded like a damned good time.

My cellphone buzzed in my pocket once again. Fucking Alex. I pulled the device from my pocket and considered ignoring him again. I didn't have time for him, but if I knew my stepbrother, and I did, if I ignored him much longer, he'd send some annoying twat of a detective looking for me again.

I reluctantly answered. "What?"

"Where the fuck are you?" Alex didn't waste time with niceties any more than I did, which was the only good quality he possessed as far as I was concerned.

"Still in Vegas." I set the phone on the table and picked up the diamonds. It probably wasn't going to take the Feds long to figure out they were fake, at which point they'd come for Nova, and by extension—me.

"Jesus. What the hell for? I thought you said your business there was going to take a day or two, tops."

"Plans change." And that was all the information I intended to give him. From day one of my father's marriage to his mother, Alex had made it abundantly clear he wanted nothing to do with their business. As if they'd trust him or any other outsider with the inner workings of what we did. As enforcers for the family, my father and I basically killed people for a living. My sissy billionaire stepbrother didn't have the stomach for that kind of work.

Although there had been a moment in Singapore where I'd thought he might take his revenge against the man who'd kidnapped his wife. He'd found a far crueler method than an easy bullet to the brain. I'd been impressed.

"That sounds like Ronin speak for *I've found a new game that probably involves fucking some people over* or worse."

I wasn't going to confirm or deny that accusation. That Alex knew me so well was disturbing enough, I didn't need to encourage him.

"Is there a point to this call? Or do you just miss me?"

Alex snorted, causing me to smile. Yanking his chain was one of my favorite pastimes. "You wish. But we do have a problem."

I found that hard to believe. We did not run in the same circles on a personal *or* professional level. It made it much easier to get along.

"What kind of problem?" I asked, although my attention to this conversation was already waning. I had millions of dollars' worth of diamonds in my hand and a pissed-off woman in the kitchen still slamming her way through the cabinets. As much as she seemed to enjoy taking orders in the bedroom, out of it, she did nothing but defy every suggestion ever made to her. Another more stubborn woman, I had not met.

And for some reason, I took that as a challenge.

"Your father is being a pain in my ass. You need to get back here and do something about him."

I barked out a laugh. "As if I have any control over that old bastard. What did he do this time?" I didn't really care, but humoring Alex might be the only way to get him off my back long enough to end this call.

"He's decided to overshare with my mother about what the two of you are up to, and now, she's about to lose her mind. A fake fiancée and blood diamonds? That better be some kind of fucking punchline to a joke I don't get."

My blood ran cold. How the fuck? I had not informed anyone of my plans. I shoved the diamonds into my pocket as if somehow Alex could see them and taking them out of sight would make the thought of them disappear.

"That is none of your fucking business."

"It absolutely shouldn't be. But when Constantine runs his mouth off to *my* mother, who can keep nothing to herself, we've all got to deal with the problem. Now, tell me exactly what this mess is about, so I can make it go away."

That matter-of-fact, all-business tone from my stepbrother grated on my last fucking nerve. The condescending asshole could take his concern and shove it up his lily-white ass. As much as I wanted to say those words, I held my tongue. I'd learned the hard way over the years that antagonizing Alex, while fun, would prolong his involvement, and in this case, I didn't want him anywhere near this situation. He might be brilliant when it came to running his global empire, but he had no clue what it took to work for the family.

"I'll handle my father."

"And my mother? What am I supposed to tell her?"

"Tell her Constantine was drunk. That shouldn't be too hard to believe."

"He has been hitting it rather hard lately. Is there something going on I need to know about?"

My blood was beginning to boil."How about

you worry about your business, and I worry about mine?"

"I'd be happy to, if your illegal bullshit didn't keep interfering in my world. You think I like this shit?"

I could feel the corners of my mouth lift in a snarl. As much as I wanted to tell him where to go, I didn't want to add any fuel to whatever brotherly internal fire crap he had going on. We were not a real family.

In fact, about the only time we'd got along is when we both decided the man who kidnapped his wife needed to be punished. Which reminded me that I had Nova to contend with. My future bride needed to be brought back under control.

"I don't really care what you like. I'll talk to Constantine, but you and your mother should assume anything he says is the pathetic ramblings of a vengeful drunk. It's all bullshit."

"Bullshit or not, your father has proven himself a danger to us all. He needs to be taken care of."

Rage rose inside me. My father had always been a heartless bastard, but he was mine to deal with, not Alex or his useless mother. "I'll do what is necessary. But it's not your decision. Tread carefully, brother, you don't want to start a war with the family."

"This has to do with your grandfather, doesn't it? Your incessant need to avenge every perceivable wrong against you is going to be what ends you, and I'm not going to be able to clean up that kind of mess."

"Sometimes, you are such an idiot. It's not about revenge— that's your poison. This is about honor and blood. Something you clearly need a lesson in. But not from me. Go fuck your wife, and leave my business to me."

I could practically hear him grinding his teeth across the phone line. The Whitman name carried a lot of power in the business world, but it meant nothing in the face of our organization.

"Fuck you, Ronin. I'll try and talk my mother down, but I'm not making any promises. She's freaked out."

I merely grunted. We both knew that he would handle her with ease. Now, I needed to figure out what my play would be. My father would have to be handled, but I needed to finish this mission first. My previously leisurely timeline had narrowed considerably.

I had to pick up the pace. I didn't want to lose

the fun of it, but the seriousness of my father's action couldn't be held at bay for long.

"What's going on?"

Nova emerged from the kitchen with a tray of meats, cheeses, olives, and crusty French bread. She also carried a full bottle of wine in her opposite hand. She took all of it to the dining table, and after grabbing two wine glasses from the bar and a bottle opener, she took a seat, tucking her feet underneath her. She seemed to be making herself entirely too comfortable, and that wasn't acceptable.

"I had a business call to take." I had no intention of sharing my family drama with this woman. I still hadn't made up my mind about what to do with her. Although I did like that I had options. The idea of keeping her dangling entertained me.

"What the hell are you doing?"

"I'm hungry and this tray was sitting in your refrigerator untouched. Aren't you hungry?"

I was, but that wasn't the point. "You should have asked. This isn't your home."

She frowned, some of the little remaining light in her eyes going dim. "It's not your house either. But if you have a problem with me eating your food,"—she popped an olive into her mouth before she continued—"I'll order another and have it delivered to you immediately."

"That won't be necessary."

She grinned at me and began her struggle to open the wine bottle. I leaned forward and swiped both the bottle and the opener from her hands.

"Hey!" She complained. "What the hell? Are you going to tell me I can't have the wine either? I'm not an eight-year-old child, you know."

"Then don't pout like or sass like one." I twisted the screw into the cork and worked the levers until the stopper popped out. "I don't mind sharing my food or wine with you, but you should ask first. It's a matter of boundaries between you and I, and I think they are important."

She defiantly popped another olive into her mouth and stared at me. Suddenly, I had a very strong urge to pull her over my knee and spank the hell out of her. Preferably until she cried—huge, wet tears—and begged me for forgiveness.

"What are you saying, Ronin? You've got rules, and as your fiancée, I'm expected to follow them? Because you should know now, I suck at following rules."

"You had no problem doing whatever your

cop lover asked of you. Hell, you didn't even care who the fuck he was, as long as he got you off, right?"

She choked and coughed, clearly unable to catch her breath.

I smiled at her, pleased that I finally had her attention.

"That's unfair. I didn't know because I didn't want to know. That doesn't make me ignorant, it makes me human."

"No, it makes you fucking stupid." This was the part where she would try and justify her actions, and I couldn't begin to care about her excuses. "There's no telling what information you may have divulged to him in the throes of passion. You should be dead already for that kind of betrayal." I let my words sink in as I poured two glasses of wine.

"Is that your plan, then? Kill me? Then why the hell did you stop my father? He could have done the job for you, and this farce would all be over."

Her starchy backbone and inability to concede both infuriated me and turned me on. I was having a hard time keeping my mind on business when I thought about all the things I could do with her sassy mouth. It was my turn to stiffen my spine and remember what was at stake here. There wasn't as much time to indulge as I'd planned for.

It was time to move up the timeline.

"We're getting married in three days."

CHAPTER 2

Rock

I threaded the needle into the jagged skin of my father's arm. He'd shown up at my apartment looking like he'd gone ten rounds in a boxing ring and then got fed through a meat grinder. This particular cut was the nastiest. It could have been from a knife, but it looked more like something jagged had done the job. Probably a piece of broken glass.

"I still think you should go to a professional to get this stitched up. I guarantee my work is going to leave a scar."

JD, my father, and the Sins of Wrath motorcycle club president, narrowed his eyes at me and grunted. "You may not have noticed, since you haven't bothered to come home in a very long time, but I have plenty of scars, already. What's one fucking more?"

It was true. Both statements. I'd hightailed it out of my hometown of Sultan, Washington a very long time ago and had no desire to ever return. And despite the blood still covering his skin and clothes, I could see the scarred tissue that seemed to crisscross his chest, arms and back. It worked around him like a road map of the life he led in a motorcycle club. A life I left behind for a reason.

I remained silent and stitched up the deep cut. If he didn't care about scars or infection, who was I to give him shit? "You shouldn't have come here."

"Why? Because you're a freaking Fed? Worried I might lead some bad motherfuckers to your lair?" He swiped the open bottle of tequila I'd left on the counter for him and took several long pulls before slamming it back down on the granite. "I'm not dumb enough to be followed, and neither are the rest of us."

I glanced around the room at his motley crew of gang-bangers. This was precisely why I had refused to take on motorcycle club cases. They hit too close to home and it was inevitable that one day this club would land on my doorstep uninvited. "I'm not worried about me. But this place *is* surveilled for my safety. Which means I'm going to have to explain your presence."

"Tell them it's a fucking family reunion. Or did you manage to leave that juicy tidbit off your job application?" he sneered.

"We both know I had to endure an intense background check before they let me step one foot near Quantico." The fact that they did, and I'd passed, was a minor miracle in and of itself.

JD snorted. "I know you don't believe that, because I didn't raise a fool. Your background is precisely why they *did* let you in. They put that shit in the bank, knowing one day they'd come back to cash out."

He wasn't wrong, but it wasn't something I wanted to dwell on. So instead, I kept my distance. The less I associated with the Sins of Wrath the more likely the brass would forget the association. Now they were about to get a big glaring reminder.

"I'm happy to help you get patched up, but then you and the boys gotta leave. No offense, but being here with me is going to put a big-ass target on your back, and I can't afford to deal with that right now."

"Too late. In case you didn't notice. Cullotta jumped me just to send you a message. We didn't plan on this, but the damage is done, and we're in it, whether you agree with that or not."

I let loose with a heavy sigh. I wasn't going to win this argument, but that didn't mean I had to make it easy for him either. Never had I met a more stubborn man than James Dean Monroe.

"I'm not dialing you in. If anything, you'll be in the way."

JD brushed my hand away from his arm. "That's too bad son, because we are definitely not going away. You're going to have to adapt and overcome."

"I'm not a fucking soldier. That's not how I operate." He was beginning to seriously piss me off, and that wasn't helping. "It's one thing to help you out in a pinch, but what you're talking about goes above and beyond."

"Son, these are extenuating circumstances. Cullotta attacked our club in your name. I can't let that go."

"Can't or won't?" Although what difference did my name make? I wasn't a club member. I'd

FALLEN ANGEL

walked away and burned the bridge down on my way out.

"It doesn't matter. Fact is, we're in it, and we aren't going away. We can either work together, or we'll go around you. What will that do to whatever operation you've got cooking?"

Fucking ruin it. I had enough irons in the fire without adding babysitting the club to the list. I'd never be able to keep up. "What did you have in mind? I can tell you right now, a war is not in the cards. I'll have you all arrested to keep that from happening."

JD shook his head. "Look around you, boy. There is a war already raging. Some of my men were shot. And we didn't go down clean. Not all Cullotta's men made it out. They aren't going to let that go."

"Shit," I cursed under my breath, barely banking the rage that rose up. He was right. Of course he was. My father always was. His ability to see and strategize was unparalleled. His help could be invaluable *if* the price wasn't too high.

"Exactly. Now let's talk about what's going to happen next."

"You're going to rest and give yourself some time to recover," I stated hopefully, despite knowing it would never happen.

He scoffed. Snickers from the other men followed. Like it or not, I'd lost the battle the minute they'd knocked on my door. "Cullotta has clearly bitten off more than he can chew," I started. "The idea that he would go after the club and think that would get me to back off shows just how desperate he has become."

Every man in the room nodded in agreement. "You must be getting too close. Got any idea what he's worried about?"

My mind immediately went to the bag of diamonds safely tucked away in my freezer. And yes, I was fully aware of how ironic it was for the diamonds to be sitting on ice. But when the knock at my door had come, I'd had to move quickly. I didn't want to share any details about my case, but that in particular seemed too risky.

"I've been seeing his daughter. Her and I are —" I didn't finish the sentence because I didn't know where we stood at this point. Well, I knew what I wanted, but getting her on the same page was going to take a little more effort.

"Fucking?" he asked.

I refused to dignify that question with an answer. Let him draw his own damned conclusions. "Listen to me, old man, because I'm only saying this once. My relationship with Nova is off limits. Although her arranged fiancé is going to be a problem."

JD whistled."Yeah, those mafia types tend to be a little possessive over their princesses. Their pussies are usually worth a lot of money."

I clenched my fists at my sides and reminded myself that JD was just stating the obvious. It wasn't personal. Mobsters did marry their daughters off as business transactions all the time. Female consent meant nothing to them.

"I think in this case it's a little more complicated. But it is still the gist of it. Although her fiancé seems to hate her father as much as we do. Not sure why he'd want to marry her. It certainly can't be just about the money. What Cullotta has pales in comparison to the Kavanaughs." He'd been thinking out loud, but he could see his father and the other club members digesting his words. He hated to admit it, but having his father as a sounding board for this case might not be all bad. The man was fucking brilliant.

"Tel." JD pointed a finger at one of his men. I didn't recognize this one, but I'd stopped keeping track of the club some years ago. Letting that go had been the final step in putting my past behind me.

"On it, Prez," he responded, grabbing a

computer from the backpack at his feet. "Wifi password?" he asked, and then paused. "Oh. Never mind."

I could see from the way the other man's fingers flew across the computer keyboard he knew exactly what he was doing. The club had a fucking hacker now? What the hell would happen next? Were they into using fucking bitcoin too?

"I'm in."

I definitely did not want to know what he was into. I doubted anything that man did with his computer fell under the "legal" umbrella. This whole situation continued to go sideways on me. I turned back to JD, ignoring whatever was happening with the hacker.

"Don't worry, Rock. Intel knows what he's doing. No one will be able to trace anything he does, and it definitely won't lead back to you."

"Just stop talking." The likelihood that my apartment was bugged was unlikely, but that didn't mean we needed to have a live conversation with details that could get us both into hot water.

"So, what else? There has to be more to this than a little dicking. Have you fallen in love with this woman? Is that why you don't want to walk away?"

I could have choked JD for that question. Nova was none of his business. She was mine, but I didn't need to beat my chest and punch something to prove it. I wasn't a caveman.

Although she might disagree with my self assessment. I could still see the hurt and anger in her eyes when she learned the truth about me. The fact that she didn't let me explain still stung. Although not as much as learning she had those diamonds. I still had a lot of questions about how that came to be.

While it was good they were now safely in my possession, if her father learned she had them—

Fuck.

"What's wrong?" JD asked.

The sudden memory of a conversation between Cullotta and his second in command must have been written all over my face. They'd talked about an airport surveillance video from the night those diamonds went missing. If he got his hands on that, then she was in more danger than anyone understood.

There seemed to be no love lost between the father and his daughter, so finding out she foiled his attempt to get his hands on those gems would be a betrayal. I doubted her position would save her from her father's wrath.

"I've got to go." I swiped my keys from the countertop. "I'd suggest it's time for you to go home, but I doubt you'll take that advice."

JD nodded. "Yep."

"Then I guess, make yourselves at home until I get back."

"We can go with you," he suggested. "Be your backup."

I snorted. "You can barely stand up, old man."

Someone sucked in their breath, while the rest of the room went deathly quiet.

"I'm not too old to put you in your place, you little shit."

There it was. The JD I remembered well. As much as my brother assured me he'd changed, so far, I'd seen nothing but more of the same. Egos the size of Cadillacs and penises the size of...

I sighed. "I don't have time for this bullshit. I'm sorry if you don't want to stay on the sidelines, but for once, you're going to do what I want. I'm not going to watch you kill anyone on my watch. And I'm not covering up for the club again. So let it go. Or let me go, and hang loose here until I get back. If you can do that, then maybe we can talk seriously about what role the club can take in all of this."

It was interesting to watch the different shades of anger cross my father's face while he tried to rein in his temper. I understood the need for revenge as much as the next guy, but this situation called for delicacy instead of brute force. There were too many unknown players at the moment.

"I'm going to cut you some slack for talking to me like that this one time. But when you get back, I'm going to kick your ass for the hell of it."

I shook my head as I headed for the door. Old man was crazy and that's all there was to it. And supposedly the apple doesn't fall far from the tree.

Which was another worry for another day.

"Where the fuck is she?" I growled my question into the comm in my ear loud enough for everyone to hear. Our search for Nova had come up empty. She wasn't in her suite, her store, with any of her friends, and she didn't show up for her usual nightcap in the hotel bar.

"No sign of her yet, boss." My new stealth

team, which consisted of two part-time guys, sounded as frustrated as me. They'd spent the entire night, well into the early morning hours scouring the city for my woman. Not exactly the focus of our investigation, but it was all related. If Cullotta took Nova, things were guaranteed to go sideways. And I wasn't sure I would remain impartial.

"What about Cullotta? Anything there?" I tapped my foot waiting for an answer. My patience had worn out hours ago. Not to mention the burning in my gut that meant nothing good when it came to this operation.

"It's been a while since anyone has laid eyes on him, but as far as we know, he's still at his compound."

"As far as you know? What the hell does that mean? Don't we still have audio on his residence?"

"That's a negative. As of an hour ago, that warrant expired. We were forced to turn it all off."

"What? I thought we were expecting an emergency extension. This is fucking urgent!" I knew yelling at the messenger wasn't going to help, but what the fuck kind of ineptness had taken over the agency? They were better than this.

"You want the facts or my opinion?" Judy, one of the best field operatives I'd worked with over the years, broke into the conversation. She normally kept so quiet on these things, I often forgot she was there. At least until we needed her, and then she always came through.

"I'll take both." I trusted her gut almost as much as my own.

"The facts are, we have everything we normally need to keep that warrant going, and yet, we've been shut down. Which leads to my opinion that either Cullotta has made himself a nice deal that we aren't privy to, or we have a problem we aren't yet aware of."

She was right. The kind of roadblocks we were hitting didn't make sense. The fact that I'd been tasked with taking this investigation underground all but screamed the obvious answer. Cullotta had gotten into bed with more of this city's leadership than should have been possible. Which left very few people I could trust. Judy, I'd stake mine and Nova's life on. And since she'd recommended Carl, and we'd both dealt with him in the past, our small team was as tight as I could get it.

Although now I had the MC to contend with. It had been hours since I'd left JD and his crew behind, and while the alarms had not indicated any traffic in or out of his apartment, I knew they were out here somewhere conducting their own investigation. My security was pretty good, but I felt it safe to assume JD's hacker buddy could make mincemeat of it.

I twisted my wrist and looked down at my watch. It wouldn't be long before we knew for certain if Nova was officially missing. She had planned a call for all her employees and contractors at the auditorium in less than an hour. Intercepting her there seemed my best bet. If not, then we'd regroup at the Sinclair, and fuck it, I would unleash the club on Cullotta.

CHAPTER 3

Nova

"*E*xcuse me?" I'd heard him loud and clear, but I couldn't believe he'd uttered those words. Was he mad?

"I'm certain I don't need to repeat myself. The arrangements are already in progress. All you need to do is pick out a dress and be ready to go on time."

I jumped from the chair. "I'm not marrying you in three days. Are you crazy? My fashion show is in three days." I looked down at my phone sitting on the table. "Well, actually it's in two and a half days, and at this point, I can't even get a good night's sleep before I have to meet my staff downstairs for our final run-through and the last one thousand details that still need to be addressed. So not no, but fuck no."

"You are a mouthy little thing," he said, his voice cold and rather emotionless. It sent a cold chill running along my spine. "If you can't be respectful when you speak to me, I'd be happy to teach you some manners."

"I don't need manners, I need my freedom." In the heat of the moment, I'd thought sending Rock away and agreeing to this farce of a marriage was the best and only choice I had. But from the moment Agent Reed left my suite, Ronin had transformed.

First, he'd insisted we move to his suite, and instead of following my instincts to say no, I'd led him lead me away from the safety of my own place to this—well, it felt suddenly like a prison.

"You traded your freedom for your life. It's as fair a bargain as you could get."

"I'm not marrying you in three days." I told him, not caring what he'd do to me. "We need to wait one more day. I have too much riding on that show. One more day shouldn't kill you."

Standing stock still, except for his eyes moving up and down my body, he unnerved me.

FALLEN ANGEL

I fought my need to squirm and nearly lost the battle when he finally picked up the two glasses of wine, carried them around the table, and handed me one of them.

"I will agree to postpone until after the show."

Thank God. Maybe he could be reasonable after all.

"On one condition."

My stomach sank. I had a hunch I wasn't going to just dislike that condition, I was going to hate it. "I'm not sleeping with—"

"Don't be crass, darling. I don't have to make bargains for sex. Besides, I prefer when my women beg, as you will, when the time is right. No. I want something entirely different from you." He took the seat next to mine and sipped his wine.

The notion of him toying with me crossed my mind. It seemed like Ronin always wanted to play some sort of game, and tonight would be no different. And I wasn't going to touch that comment about making his women beg no matter how much he baited me to react.

"What do you want then?" I asked, hoping I didn't regret asking. If I couldn't give him what he wanted…. Well, I had to give him what he wanted, didn't I? The condition of my show

31

going off this week was more important than anything else, including my dignity.

"Answers."

Now that I did not see coming. "About what? I hate to tell you, but I probably don't know as much as you think I do. My life these days consists of work and more work." That had been true until I met Rock. Then my life had changed. Not that I needed to remind Ronin of that. He already knew too many of the intimate details about my love life.

"Trust me. You'll have these. And if not, then no fashion show. I'm a simple man, so I will make this as easy as possible."

I doubted he had a simple bone in his body, but I wasn't going to say that. He wanted manners, I'd give them to him. At least as long as I could. "Go on," I urged.

"Only two questions. First, how did you get your hands on those diamonds? You don't strike me as a thief, let alone one knowledgeable enough to get those. Did you pay someone for them?"

I smiled at that. Did it matter if he knew? I quickly decided that it did not. He'd watched me throw them at Rock and they were no longer mine.

"That would have been the smart thing to do, but then someone else would have known I had them, and I wasn't willing to go there." More lies I couldn't afford for him to figure out. My sister knew.

He leaned back in his chair, and eyed me warily. "Are you trying to tell me that you actually stole them yourself? I find that hard to believe. Let me remind you that this agreement between us only works if you are honest. Otherwise, we're done talking, and I'll make arrangements for us to leave now."

Panic seized me. I had no doubt Ronin would resort to kidnapping if that's what it took to get his way. "I am being honest. They were smuggled into the country on board Vincent Cabrini's plane on his last trip to Italy. My father and his father cooked up the whole damn plan. Once I knew that, it wasn't as hard as you'd think to gain access. Although that part I did pay for. Luckily, private planes are still given a lot of leeway at airports, despite tighter international security. After that, it was just a matter of search and seizure. There are only so many places to hide something like that and still be able to access it."

He set the wine glass down on the table and steepled his fingers in front of his face. "You expect me to believe it was really that easy? You waltzed onto a celebrity's private plane, searched it, found the diamonds, and then waltzed back off without a care in the world."

I lifted my brows and smirked at him. "It was definitely not *that* easy. Simple in plan yes, but it still took a lot of finesse, research, and timing before I could pull it off. I had to study schematics of that plane ahead of time, not only so I had ideas on where to look, but also because I wouldn't have a lot of time. Information is the key to an operation such as that. Then I had to locate the right people to bribe at the airport, and then get in and out of there without anyone seeing me."

"Then you were lucky."

"Probably. I took as many precautions as I could, but there were no guarantees. What good thing in life happens without at least a little luck?"

"You might be right." He pushed from the chair and paced across the room. "However, I still can't decide whether I should be impressed with your skills as a thief or your skills as an actress who is probably lying to me."

"I don't think I would make a good actress," I

FALLEN ANGEL

blurted, sprinting very close to the line of desperation. I needed him to believe me.

He turned towards me and grasped the back of one of the dining chairs before leaning forward and narrowing his eyes. "We shall see."

What the hell was that supposed to mean?

"Second and last question. "What really happened the night you left your father's house? Why were you exiled so completely from your family that he let you run wild and free these last five years unchecked?"

Oh shit. This was bad. Really bad.

I did my best to school the shock, but his question had been the equivalent of a gut punch and I could tell by the rise of his eyebrows that he'd caught my initial reaction.

"Let me remind you that anything less than the complete truth is unacceptable. Think hard here if your fashion show is worth the price of your lies."

Dammit. I was stuck between a rock and a hard place. If I told him the truth, I could be opening a whole lot of trouble I couldn't handle. On the other hand, if I didn't tell him, he'd make sure my dreams went up in a fiery death. There was no doubt in my mind he could do it, too. His

35

reputation aside, I'd seen firsthand how devious he could actually be. Or so I'd thought...

"You're asking me to betray an oath I made to my father. To do so would only prove that I couldn't be trusted—to him and to you."

He shrugged. "I don't care if you betray your father, although I do see your point. Once a traitor always a traitor. Isn't that right, Catherine?"

The sound of my real name on his lips unnerved me. He probably knew more about my life than I did. So what was the point of this little exercise? Although the death of my first husband had not been made public, to my knowledge. My father had promised that while some would speculate, the facts would never surface. And he'd been right. I'd not heard even a whisper about it.

"So you are going to hold it against me know matter which way I go? Damned if I do and damned if I don't."

Again, his shoulder lifted in an expression that clearly said he didn't care about my predicament. "But what choice do you have? You can either give me the information I seek or live with the consequences."

"You're an asshole." So much for manners.

"That may be true, but it changes nothing." The corners of his mouth lifted slightly. "Besides, why fight the inevitable? We both know you're going to tell me exactly what I want to know."

I clenched the fingers on my right hand. I had never wanted to punch something so badly as I wanted to hit him in that moment. I would have given almost anything to wipe that smug smile off his face. I wasn't much for hate, but he inspired it. I hated him with every fiber of my being. He was going to toy with me until the bitter end, and I knew it.

And yet...I was going to do exactly what he said I would.

"My eighteenth birthday was a straight up nightmare." I had blocked most of the memories over the years, and even managed to stop seeing it in my nightmares. The one thing I had not done was forget. No. That night would forever be burned into my brain because it was the night I learned I, too, could be a monster.

Just like my father.

"Knowing your father, I would expect nothing less."

I frowned. "Well, that makes one of us. When I was summoned to his office, just as the party got started, I had no idea what was about to

E.M. GAYLE

happen. My mother told me nothing about what was expected of me."

He slowly shook his head. "I will never understand parents who aren't willing to train their children. It's the least they can do."

A near laugh burst from between my lips. "My mother cares about no one other than her sons. Well, and her reputation. She has been and always will be obsessed with her station in life and how she is perceived. It's disgusting. And if I hadn't already understood that, I certainly would have that night. She and my father ambushed me with a man they insisted I had to marry that night."

"But you didn't marry. How in the hell did you get out of it?"

He sounded genuinely curious and equally certain that I had never married. That was probably the bill of goods my father sold him. Not a virgin, but never married, either. Making a marriage to me seem more palpable. All lies.

"I didn't. Although not for lack of trying. I negotiated, cajoled, and even begged for more time. Unfortunately, I might as well have been talking to a wall. My father refused to listen."

"Excuse me?"

Those two words came out on a vicious hiss

of anger that didn't bode well for anyone, least of all me.

"He forced me to marry that night, while my high school friends partied yards away inside the main house. I could hear the laughter and the music spilling from the ballroom as I vowed to love, honor and obey a stranger old enough to be my grandfather."

Ronin's knuckles turned white from his grip on the back of the chair until I thought the wood would break. Instead, he jerked the chair free from under the table and flung it across the room. I jerked at the crack of it against the wall, feeling the rage as if it were my own. Absolutely nothing he could say or feel would be as bad as what I experienced that night. As my new husband climbed on top of our marital bed, and my fear paralyzed me from stopping him.

"He's dead, isn't he?"

I didn't have to ask who he meant. I nodded as the broken memories attempted to unfurl in my mind, reminding me one final time that my current fiancé was not the only monster in the room.

CHAPTER 4

Nova

*ive years ago*

"I can't do this," I whispered to my mother, who'd maintained a firm hold on me throughout the entire ceremony. "I'm not feeling well. I think I'm going to throw up."

"Whining to me or your father is not going to work." My mother loosened her death grip on me, and I slumped back against the wall to stop myself from falling. I still couldn't believe this was happening.

My father scowled at me as he moved closer and out of ear shot of the others. "I shouldn't have to repeat myself, but I can see you're not yourself, so I'll explain it once again. Mr. Onofrio was particularly interested in your specific attributes, and paid handsomely for the privilege of being your first. So our end of the deal is not fulfilled until he has broken the seal, so to say. However, it is a done deal. This will happen tonight if I have to tie you down to the bed myself."

My stomach churned, threatening a true revolt. I didn't know why I thought more lies would change a thing, but they sprang forth nonetheless. If nothing else, I could make him hurt where it counted the most. His wallet.

"If that's the case, then this definitely is going to be a problem. You probably should have verified the goods before you sold them, because I'm not what you seem to think I am."

His eyes narrowed again to barely a squint. We both knew what I was talking about, but I could see he would need me to spell it out.

"I'm not a virgin," I lied. "That ship sailed a while ago."

FALLEN ANGEL

I held perfectly still watching the anger build in my father. This was not the conversation I'd ever dreamt of having with the man I once called daddy. I might be young, but I knew enough to realize this moment was going to hurt for a very long time. He had sold me like a piece of furniture, and agreed to let this man do with me what he wanted.

The muscle in his jaw clenched as I waited for the explosion. He turned away from me and looked at my mother. "Is this true?"

"I have no idea. I've never seen her so much as talk to a boy. I would have told you." Her voice trembled with fear, and for a second, guilt washed over me. If he blamed her…

"Those fucking terms were non-negotiable," he hissed. "You had better be lying, because if you're not, and that old bastard can tell the difference and demands a refund, you are fucked my dear. You will spend the rest of your life on your back, working off the debt to any man who will still touch you."

My lip curled at the father I no longer recognized.

The fact he only wanted a virgin bride sickened me. I was surprised he bothered to wait for one who was legal.

43

E.M. GAYLE

"Let's not go there, yet. This information can be verified. It will only delay us for a short time." Then she turned to me. "If this is true, and you have shamed your family in this way, you will only get what you deserve."

I shuddered to think what that might be. Not to mention the idea that he would have it *verified*.

When he picked up his phone and pressed it to his ear, I didn't know what to do.

"Francisco, I need you to bring my doctor to my office." He nodded at whatever his man said. "Yes. Right now."

He ended the call and calmly placed his phone back on his desk. "If you are no longer a virgin as you say, then I will give you to Francisco. He has a fondness for whores he can fuck and torture. Besides, I have another daughter..."

My mother gasped, but my father did not spare her a glance. My own stomach churned. Carina was barely thirteen. He couldn't be serious. He wouldn't dare.

I stared back at him. His eyes colder than I'd ever seen. He saw through my lies, but he also wanted me to know that whatever deal he'd struck with this man was more important than either of us. If it wasn't me, it would be her, and I couldn't let that happen.

44

I hung my head in defeat. There was no way to fight this. He would get his way, one way or another.

"I don't have to see a doctor," I whispered.

"Excuse me?" He said. "I didn't hear you."

I lifted my head and straightened my spine. If I was going to do this it wouldn't be as a meek little girl. "I said I don't need a doctor. I lied."

"Catherine, what is wrong with you?" My mother shrieked. Before I saw it coming, she slapped my face with a resounding crack. Pain exploded in my cheek. Tears pooled in my eyes as I cupped my burning face.

"Take her to the bedroom, and prepare her for her new husband. We have some final paperwork to sign."

She grabbed me again and all but hauled me out of the chair and in the direction of the door. Betrayal of immeasurable magnitude filled every cell of my body as she dragged me into the other room and practically threw me in the direction of the bed.

"You have been nothing but trouble since the day you were born. I tried to tell him you would not go quietly. But this is too far. Do you hear me? Too far."

"Why do you hate me so much?" My mother

had never been kind, but I'd never experienced anything quite like this. Not even when she whipped me for breaking one of her many rules.

"You were my firstborn, and you should have been a boy. It was expected of me. Until your brother came along, you were a constant shame to me. After," she hesitated. "I no longer needed you."

The cold shiver that rippled through me at her words threatened to tear me in two. It was one thing to assume she hated me, another to hear it as truth. Her heartless words did what her and my father's demands could not. In that moment, I gave up. I let the pain wash over me and numb me to the fear drowning me.

I accepted this night as my fate, and promised myself if I could survive this marriage, then the next would be everything I could hope for.

"WHAT DO you mean he had a heart attack?!" My mother shrieked. "That does not look like a heart attack."

Her hysteria wasn't unwarranted. The virginal white gown she'd given me to wear for my wedding night was covered in my dead husband's blood.

I'd woken with a headache and a desperate need to vomit. At first, I didn't know where I was or who I was with, until bits and pieces of the wedding and aftermath came back to me. I climbed out of the bed and ran into the bathroom, my mouth covered. By the time I finished retching and cleaned up, I didn't bother with a light since I had no desire to look myself in the eye. The shame of it all. I had no idea how I would ever look at myself again.

It wasn't until I returned to the bedroom, I realized something was truly wrong. A sliver of light through the heavy curtains fell across the middle of the bed. I almost didn't look for fear I would throw up again.

But the red, across my mother's pristine white sheets flashed in my peripheral vision, and I had to investigate. My body jerked backward at what I saw. The man. My husband. He was lying in the middle of the bed with a knife buried in the middle of his chest. Blood everywhere.

I didn't remember screaming, but Francisco had come running. From there, it had all played out in slow motion as I stood, unable to move until my mother arrived, angry and vocal that she had been woken from her much needed beauty sleep.

"Shut up," my father said, his face contorted in anger as well. "I said it was a heart attack, and that's what it was. The man was in his seventies and not exactly a picture of health. It will come as no surprise.

"But—"

"What, Sandra? Do you want me to tell everyone the truth? That your daughter murdered her husband on their wedding night? What do you think will happen after that?"

My mother gasped.

I closed my eyes and wished for death myself. Overnight, I'd gone from clueless teenager to this. A monster. Just like them.

Just like them.

"What are we going to do?"

"*We* aren't going to do anything. If this ever comes up, we will claim he had a heart attack or a stroke."

"But he has a hole—"

"Enough. Don't make me repeat myself. Go back to the house and stay with the children, Sandra. I will handle this. Francisco!" my father bellowed toward the door.

My father's most trusted foot soldier entered

FALLEN ANGEL

again, his face hard and unemotional. He was always at the ready to serve at my father's whim. "Yes, Sir?" he asked, looking only at my father, and behaving as if it was just another day of work at the office. I had no doubt whatever he was asked to do, he would, no questions asked.

"Please see that my wife returns to the house and stays with the other children. Assign more security to watch over them and then come back here. As for—*her*,"—he practically spat the word at me with pure disgust, cementing the guilt and horror running through my mind. "Make sure she and this room are cleaned up and then escort her to the house. She is leaving today and will be taking only two suitcases with her. She is to be given a plane ticket to the city of her choice and one thousand dollars. Not a penny more. And then escorted to the airport. Is that understood?"

His words finally caught my attention as I turned and stared at him in shock. What was he saying?

"Don't look so surprised, Catherine. You can't stay here. You have brought immeasurable shame on your family and enough trouble for me that it will take me years to untangle it all. Be glad I'm not just throwing you out in the cold with nothing or worse, calling the police. A life-

49

E.M. GAYLE

time in jail would be no picnic, I assure you. No, count your blessings that I have given you this reprieve. You can have the freedom you wanted after all—for a while. When the time is right for your return, I will contact you, at which time, you will return and serve your family as intended.

"I want at least five years."

Why that random number popped into my head I didn't know.

"Dearest daughter, I don't believe you have any room to negotiate with me." He practically sneered his response, and it triggered something inside of me.

"But don't I? If the truth came out, it would hurt you as much as me." Hopefully, the words came out like I intended. My brain couldn't seem to focus. I shook my head to try and clear it before I continued. "If I have to leave the only family I have known and can expect no support beyond what I leave the house with, then I think five years is more than fair." I clutched my hands behind my back so he wouldn't see them shake.

He stared at me silently, his face pinched in anger while he seemed to think about my offer.

"Five years, ten years, what does it matter?" my mother asked. "We don't need her anymore."

Something vile formed on the end of my tongue, and by sheer will I held it in. My mother no longer existed to me, and I would not waste another minute of my time on her.

"I'm the one who decides how this goes. Anything I give you is a gift you should thank me for. However, it is your birthday so I will grant this favor. You follow the rules, keep your mouth shut, and in five years, you will return, accepting whatever plans I have made for you with no argument. That's the deal—take it or leave it."

As much as I wanted to throw his deal back in his face, what other option did I have? Five years was a long time.

"I'll take it."

"Of course you will. And while it may be difficult, I will find a suitable husband for you so that you can serve your family as intended."

My stomach twisted at my father's final words.

"Let's go," Francisco touched my arm and I jerked away from him. He made my skin crawl.

"I don't need any assistance," I said, twisting out of his reach. I turned one last time to the man I called father. "You've underestimated me, and you definitely don't know me."

He glanced my way. "No, daughter. It is you

E.M. GAYLE

who underestimates me. I am always one step ahead of my adversaries, and it would do you good to remember that."

Instead of arguing with him further, I ran. Out of the godforsaken guest house, across the lawn, to my room, and then out the front door.

Catherine Novaline Cullotta would be no more. For as long as he allowed, I would become someone else.

And thus, Nova was born.

CHAPTER 5

Rock

After endless hours of fruitless searching, I decided to set up camp in the most likely place Nova would turn up. I'd exhausted every resource available to me to locate her and this was kind of my last chance effort. I'd been informed, rather reluctantly, by hotel management that there were several important pre-show events happening today, including a final rehearsal and some sort of VIP reception that included many members of the press. If she was able, Nova would *not* miss this.

I spotted Zia's arrival backstage, her crew of

waitstaff carrying in tray after covered tray that they set up on some of the tables just off stage. It made sense these events would be catered by the in-house restaurant and not some outside company. She and Nova were also close friends so I made a mental note to question her as soon as possible. Maybe she had some insight I could use to find Nova. Not that I wanted to alarm anyone unnecessarily that she might be missing if that was not the case.

Her assistant had assured me that the woman in question would arrive shortly, but I couldn't decide if they'd actually been in touch, or if the woman's seemingly eternal optimism refused to believe anything else.

Some of the other staff had already arrived early, and they scurried between this area and behind the curtain, placing tables and chairs as well as a myriad of glitzy decorations and flower arrangements. I didn't profess to be an expert on the fashion business, but I'd done enough research to know how critical this event would be to launch an artist's designs.

Unfortunately, there was no sign of the boss —yet. Her historical need for a perfectly punctual arrival should have had her here first, and because of the nature of my work, my mind typically went to the worst case scenario first and worked its way backwards from there. However, in this case I refused to acknowledge the pessimism eating me from the inside out.

She had to be alive.

There were a dozen different scenarios my mind could work through, but I couldn't stop thinking about just one.

Fuck.

I slammed forward at the precise moment the door nearest me opened, and Nova slipped inside. Her sudden appearance should have given me immense relief, but it lasted only a moment before anger replaced the worry. Why had she not answered any of my calls or texts? As she swept through the darkened auditorium, her dark hair cascading in the air behind her and her mask of indifference already slipped over her face, the sudden urge to do something drastic rushed over me.

Keeping her safe had become my number one priority.

I took two steps forward before a hand touched my shoulder and stopped me. "Don't"

I shoved my father's hand off me, turning on him with a snarl. "Don't touch me." The anger coursing through me had gone from red to white-hot in a flash. Gone were the even-tempered thoughts of the cop, only to be replaced by the murderous thoughts of a man in...

"Easy, son. I'm just here to talk. Thought you might like to know I saw your man sitting on Cullotta's place, although the bastard slipped him a while ago. Don't worry though, we're on him. We've got it covered."

"Right," I snapped. I could only imagine what that entailed and how long it would last before JD took measures in his own hand. "I need him alive to close this fucking case. If you kill him all the work I've done will be for nothing."

"We aren't the ones looking to kill someone right now. You need to check yourself before you go off half-cocked. That won't win you any points with her."

We both turned to Nova, now on the stage talking to a group of women huddled around her.

"Then what are you doing here?" I still didn't feel quite myself, but some of my brain cells were beginning to fire again. Enough to question JD anyways. "How in the hell did you find me anyways?"

JD snorted. "You don't think I remember

what a man desperate in love looks like? Where else would you be?"

Those were about the last words I needed to hear right now. If I stopped and examined my feelings too close, I was going to go over the edge. "Don't go there. Focus, old man, and tell me why you're really here."

He shook his head. "You're as hot-headed as you were at twenty. Figured you would have grown out of that by now."

"What can I say? You bring out the worst in me." I regretted the jab the minute it left my mouth. Getting into another fight with my father was not on my agenda, today or any day. He was right. I had grown out of it. I'd channeled all of that anger into this job, and it had served me well. It wasn't until...

When exactly had everything changed? It certainly wasn't when I met Nova. Getting to know her had been so much more than I expected. At least until—

Fucking Ronin showed up.

And I meant that figuratively and literally. The fucker crossed the stage to Nova's side and leaned in to whisper something into her ear, his hand at the small of her back in a far too intimate gesture. So much for banking the anger raging inside me. It went right back from the barely there simmer I'd managed to a full boil in two point five seconds. This was fucked up. I was supposed to walk away. She'd chosen him over me. As far as I knew they could be sleeping together by now. Another thought that sent my blood pressure careening out of control. Maybe I was going to have to kill someone. It wasn't the ideal answer to the problem, but it would be the most effective.

Ridding the world of another mafia enforcer didn't sound like a bad deal. Two or three birds with one stone actually worked out in my favor...

"So I can see part of your problem," my father interrupted my dangerous train of thought.

I shook my head, in an attempt to clear my mind. "Don't even go there. My personal life is *my* personal life. Houston sticking his nose in it is enough, I don't need you adding to that."

He laughed at that. "I was wondering if you two had gotten past your differences."

I nearly rolled my eyes. Ever since my brother had fallen in love with Izzy, he'd turned into a little bitch, insisting I didn't know what I was missing out on. "Our differences are still miles wide."

"And yet you're close enough for him to interfere in your private business." The smile across his face when he spoke made me frown. I didn't hate my father for wanting to be a father, but I wasn't entirely comfortable with it either. There were too many years between us that had created a divide that wasn't easy to cross. At least not for me. Especially not now, when my focus needed to be on the woman across the room from me and the case that was threatening to implode if I didn't figure out how to nail Cullotta before he did something that could send me over the edge.

This was not the first time I'd ridden the fine line between right and wrong, but I couldn't remember another situation that left me this —desperate.

Talk about uncomfortable. Between Nova's fiancé and her father, I suddenly had two people on a hit list that had stood empty for a dozen years.

"If you clench your fists any tighter, you're going to break your fingers. If that man is such an issue, why not do something about him?"

I turned and looked at JD. He had no idea how impossible his simplistic statement was. "Because bringing a motorcycle club shaped blow torch to the party isn't going to fix anything."

"I don't disagree that there is a time for finesse and a time for brute force. However, if your woman is in danger, then I think you know what time it is." With that, he walked away and disappeared into the shadows as quickly as he'd appeared. I had no idea where he would go or what havoc he would wreak, but I'd have to let it go for the moment. It was time for Nova and me to have a talk.

"Hey!" I whisper called after him into the dark. "Do you really want to help?" When no answer came, I wasn't entirely sure if he was still there. However, my gut said he was, so I continued. "You think your hacker can find me anything new on Ronin Kavanaugh outside the normal channels? I've exhausted what I can do with the FBI database."

I received no response. Old man still had moves. Not that I would ever underestimate him. Decades as a co-president and then president to the MC showed that the man wasn't easy to outwit. His men didn't follow him blindly, because he would never tolerate that, but they did follow him faithfully because that's what he had earned. I shrugged to myself. I'd shoot him a text and see just how serious they were about helping instead of sabotaging this situation. I'd run out of resources through normal channels, it was time to take it underground, get my questions answered, and ask for forgiveness later.

First, though, I turned my focus back to the woman on stage, she and I were going to talk. Or fight. Or fuck.

Maybe all three.

Whatever it took to get her to listen.

CHAPTER 6

Ronin

Of course the little minx had lied. I'd kept my questions for Nova simple, if not easy, and she'd given me a story that might have had some truth to it, with a heaping side of bullshit.

Although my fiancée had done a damned good job of trying to convince me that her words were true. The tears had been an especially nice touch. She didn't consider herself an actress, but as it turned out, she was a damned fine one.

Looking at her now, for example, she lorded over her staff like the beautiful, beloved queen she wanted to be. No one had a clue how precarious her life had become. As far as they were concerned, she'd built an incredible business that had exploded her into the stratosphere and they were happily riding the skies on her coattails. Without a single person realizing it was nothing more than a house of cards that was about to explode all over the Vegas strip.

And I would be the one to detonate it.

I didn't understand why she needed this fashion show so much. She already had fame and fortune. Something she'd seemingly built on her own without a cent of her father's money or any other helping hand. I guessed it would be a boost to her already booming career, but when it came to her life, she had much larger things to worry about than whether the people in this town liked a bunch of expensive dresses. Her priorities were fucked, and they needed an adjustment as soon as possible.

First, though, she would wow the world, and then I'd pull the rug out from under her.

That tale she'd woven about her first husband having a heart attack the night of their wedding had rung as false as the bullshit she fed the cop. It hadn't been easy to keep a straight face either. When the lies began, I itched to make them stop.

She had a lot to learn and soon enough she'd get it.

A heart attack. What a joke. In retrospect, his actual death meant very little. The man had been a dick to everyone he came in contact with, including his family. The lack of confirmation, however, had left a gap in their organization big enough to cause serious problems. For five years, the family had fought to maintain their position as my uncle, slowly took over the organization. It had been a bloody, prolonged war, and finally, the time had come to lay my grandfather to rest once and for all.

But her story didn't make sense. Arnald's body had never been found. Which meant that her father had gone to great effort to hide and/or dispose of it. No one needed to do that for a heart attack. No, something far more sinister had occurred, and it was my job to uncover it.

Our family had waited five long years for answers, and it wasn't until that dumbass Cullotta had offered up his daughter to our family—again—that we had finally brought the investigation to the forefront. This time, answers would be had. One way or another, and I didn't give a shit who had to die to get them. Including

E.M. GAYLE

one pretty, little minx with a penchant for not telling the truth.

"Afraid if you don't keep eyes on the little woman at all times that you won't be able to hold onto her?"

A smile crossed my face at the sudden but not unexpected appearance of Rock Reed at my side. I figured he'd be lurking around still trying to solve whatever puzzle he needed solved and chasing after a woman who belonged to me now. Although approaching me like this reeked of desperation. At this point, he wasn't much more than a useless pawn in this game, but sometimes the pawn surprised you and made the game more interesting.

"Showing support is not the same as stalking a woman who has made it clear she wants nothing to do with you. You would think there would be a better way to spend taxpayer dollars."

That seemed to rankle the cop, as he clenched and unclenched his fists several times. It could be fun if the man decided to take a swing at me, but I doubted very much he would lose control here in front of a dozen witnesses. Now, were we ever to meet alone in a dark alley, I believed it would be a different story. I'd dug up enough on him to realize he definitely had a dark side. One never knew, maybe that meeting could happen.

"What are you really doing here, Kavanaugh? We both know you don't give a shit about her."

Despite his position as a federal agent, I appreciated his direct approach. People who couldn't or wouldn't speak their mind annoyed the fuck out of me.

"You already know the answer to that. I'm sure even you understand the concept of family obligations."

The sharp swivel of his head in my direction told me that I'd hit on something rather sensitive. Interesting. Now I would have to look more into the family of one Rockford Reed, FBI agent. I had already encountered his brother Houston at Nova's birthday party, but his reaction told me I'd missed something else.

"You really expect me to believe that the most notorious mob enforcer on the East Coast as well as one of the most well-known wealthy playboys is suddenly going to settle down with a woman he doesn't know and what, start having babies, because your daddies say so? Sounds a little too punk, even for you."

I ground my teeth to keep from blurting something too telling. He obviously wanted to push my buttons. Little shit probably knew more about me than I cared for. This was why Nova had no fucking business messing around with him. We did not need this kind of heat knocking on our door at this juncture. I couldn't let him interfere with my mission here.

Instead of lobbing more sarcasm that would only fuel his fire, I remained silent. There was a time to play with and a time to study your opponent. This felt like the latter.

"If you marry her, I'm going to make it my new life's mission to take you down. She deserves better than someone like you."

I barked with laughter. "You don't like to play it very close to the vest, do you? You might as well have beat your chest and called her yours. How cliché."

He shrugged. "Only stating the obvious. Letting you know we are not done."

My laughter died. "*When* I marry her, I'm going to take her back to New York and lock her in my penthouse where she'll become nothing more than my sex slave, since she so obviously enjoys a kinky fuck. She'll serve me at my whim and wait like a good girl for when I call. And you know what? She's going to fucking love it. So much so that she'll beg for more and more and more until I've used her up and ruined her for anyone else. Maybe then, I'll send her back your way. You can see then if she's still good enough to hold your attention. Not likely would be my guess."

I kept my gaze on Nova as I let my tirade do its thing in his brain. I didn't have to see Agent Reed's face to know how angry I made him. I could feel the emotion vibrating off of him. I had probably gone too far, but he had pissed me off. I didn't appreciate him sticking his nose where it didn't belong. If he thought he was going to continue to dip his fingers in my fucking cookie jar, I was going to cut them off.

It might be the only way he'd learn that he couldn't win with me. I was not beneath him, nor were we on some sort of level playing field. As far as I was concerned, the only reason he was here was because I allowed it.

"Now we're done."

With no need for a response, I took a step forward with the intent of heading backstage where I could wait for Nova in relative quiet. I had phone calls to make and business to conduct. I'd had my fill of—

A hard grip on my arm stopped me. I swung back, jerking free from his touch. "Don't fucking touch me again," I hissed, rage seething from every cell in my body. "So far, I have allowed your interference because it has been entertaining, but trust me when I say, you do *not* want me as your enemy."

"I don't give a shit what your agenda is for me," Agent Reed seethed. "But if you fucking touch her, you. Are. Dead."

CHAPTER 7

Nova

As I flipped through my massive to-do list on my tablet, the nervous butterflies in my stomach once again revolted. There were too many outstanding details to deal with. A few of the dresses needed last minute adjustments, the seating chart had gone to shit because of some guest list changes, and there were a pile of new interview requests that I needed to contend with immediately. And that was just a few things of many more just like them. The demands of an event like this were overwhelming.

And there was everything going on that had nothing to do with this show. I closed my eyes, took a deep breath, and held it. There wasn't time for a breakdown today. Probably not tomorrow either, since I still needed to get out of this wedding and figure out how to contact my sister. And then—

"Hi."

Every muscle in my body froze at the sound of that one little word coming from behind me. The tears I'd just beaten back threatened all over again. "Rock," I whispered, feeling both terror and enormous relief at saying his name.

"We need to talk."

Now there were four words that could knock me out of this stupor. "No, we don't." I kept my face buried in the document in front of me, refusing to turn around and look at him. I may not have read a single word, but at least I wasn't looking at him. The pain of his betrayal was far too fresh. "I can't," I added. "There are a million details for me to deal with today and you cannot be one of them. You just can't."

Everything else in my world might be falling apart around me, but by God, this show would not be one of them. I would get through this day intact if it killed me. I dropped my chin to my chest at my poor choice of words. I was living in a nightmare and I needed someone to wake me up from it. Someone whose name was not Rock Reed.

"If I didn't think it was a matter of life and death, I would wait."

"No. No. No." I shook my head, trying to ignore how good he looked standing in front of me with that familiar look of yearning on his face that always brought me to my knees. He always took charge and demanded I acquiesce, but in return, he always gave so much more than he took. "You can't come in here and do this to me right now."

He stepped forward and gripped my shoulders, pulling me close enough to smell the aftershave he wore that, when mixed with his scent, was enough to drive me wild all on its own.

"I wish I could have told you who I was from the beginning. I really do. Hurting you was the last thing I wanted to do."

Hearing those words tripped something in my chest, that piece of me that I needed to keep locked away. Not that it mattered. It couldn't. Not when I couldn't see past the pain sliding through my body like an oil slick that coated everything with a blackness that was guaranteed to kill.

"You can't do this," I repeated, hating how feeble my protest sounded. "We aren't together anymore." I tore free from his grip and turned my back on him. "Not that we were ever together together, but you know what I mean."

He stepped forward again, this time not touching me, but leaving me no less unnerved as the heat emanating from his big body seeped into my needy skin.

"We were together. Are together. This is just a temporary setback."

"A setback?!" I whirled to him, renewed anger filling some of the emptiness inside me. "Are you kidding me?"

I barely had the question out when the full visual impact of him hit me in the chest and knocked the air from my lungs.

He was so beautiful. In a rugged, strong, and impossible to resist kind of way. His features were honed to perfection. From the color of his eyes, the broad nose that fit the shape of his face instead of being too big or too small, to the full ruddy lips that threatened to scramble my brain just from looking at them.

His hair had grown out quite a bit since the

night we'd met, the ends brushing the shell of his ears and it looked like he'd not bothered to shave this morning because the lower portion of his face had a thick growth of stubble that enhanced the strong set of his jaw. But it was the sight of his mesmerizing green eyes I knew were flecked with tiny bits of gold that captured my attention most. I hadn't braced for the full impact of seeing him again, and now I wasn't sure how long I could hold up under that kind of pressure.

"Maybe not the best choice of words, but I'm not feeling particularly eloquent today. I haven't had a lot of sleep and too many people are getting in my way today."

"Boo fucking hoo. We all have problems, and yours are not mine and mine are not yours. I gave you what you wanted and now all I expect in return is for you to leave me alone."

He smirked. "That's not going to happen."

I sighed, throwing up my arms. "What the hell..?" I hesitated. "This is ridiculous. I don't even know what to call you now. Agent Reed?"

"I'd prefer if you called me Rock. Well, technically I'd still like to hear Sir come from your beautiful lips again, but for now, Rock will do."

Shaking my head, I crossed the room in the opposite direction of him, putting some much needed space between us. "I can't even with you. I am surrounded by men with egos as big as this hotel, and it's infuriating."

He smiled. "Our egos are the last of your worries, sweetheart. It's our intentions you should focus on."

I narrowed my eyes, not sure how to take any of what he said. "And what are your intentions, Agent Reed?" Calling him Rock felt too intimate at this point, and it would be a cold day in hell before he heard Sir from my lips again.

"I've come to move you to a safe location. I believe you have been compromised and that your life is in danger."

His perfunctory, cryptic statements were starting to give me a headache. I took two fingers and pressed them to my forehead to relieve the throbbing behind my eyes. "Why would I be in danger? That doesn't even make sense. "

"I have reason to believe that your father has learned you took the diamonds. If he comes for them, and realizes you no longer have them in your possession, I don't think he'd be very happy. And he seems to have a hair trigger lately. There have been new reports of violence from within his organization. So, we have a safe house I can escort you to, where I can be certain you are secure. At least for now."

The blood drained from my face at the idea my father knew about me and the diamonds. If that were true, it wasn't just me in danger.

"That can't be right. I was careful. The few people who know would never tell him." My mind raced as I tried to find something that made sense.

"He doesn't need someone to tell him. Apparently, there's an airport surveillance video that may have told him for you."

"Oh shit." I thought I had covered all my bases. I'd researched the camera locations ahead of time, and made sure I avoided all of them. It had to be a mistake. This stupid nightmare was getting worse at every turn. What the hell had I been thinking? A marriage to Ronin suddenly sounded a hell of a lot easier than untangling this web of lies.

"Exactly," he said. "However, if we go now, I might be able to contain this before it grows out of control. There's a time limit, though."

I blinked at him. "I'm not going anywhere. I have too much to do here. I only have a few days left."

E.M. GAYLE

"What the fuck, Nova? Did you not hear what I just said?"

"Of course I did. But I have made promises and people are counting on me. I can't run out on that. Whatever is going to happen, it's going to have to wait until this show is over. I only need a little more time and then I can figure this out."

He looked like he wanted to throttle me. His face turned dark and his eyes flashed with anger. "We can't wait that long."

"Why not? What's a few more days in the grand scheme of things?"

"Do you think your father really gives a shit about your responsibilities? He won't wait."

"Even *my* father isn't going to try something here. Gabe has every millimeter of this building covered with security. My father is a lot of things, but stupid isn't one of them. He's not going to risk getting caught."

Before Rock could answer, his cell phone dinged, and he fished it out of his pocket. The string of curses that came from him then nearly blistered my ears. I'd never seen him so upset, and I wasn't sure how to take it.

"We're leaving now." He started toward me.

I scooted away. "No. We are not." Although I

had to admit he was scaring me, and I did not want my father anywhere near me again.

He was on me in three strides, and there wasn't a chance in hell I could win against the tight grip he wrapped around my arm.

"Let me go, right now, or I will scream assault."

That must have gotten his attention because he stilled, his fingers still digging into my arm. "You wouldn't. I don't think you want to die today, Nova."

A shudder worked down my spine. I know he referred to my father, but they came out like vicious claws meant to rake through my soul. Every syllable hitting a nerve. Rock Reed was just a man doing his job. This wasn't about me. He would do exactly the same for any other person in this situation. Only he had not been that to me. He wasn't just a hot fuck pitstop on the road to a job well done. Those weeks we had spent together meant something to me. They had changed me.

If I couldn't find a way to preserve those memories, how were they going to sustain me through the coming nightmare?

As much as I hated to admit it, I was stuck in a dark place. Unable to forget, or even set aside, the fact that he'd used me. I'd been nothing more than a source of information. How was I ever going to see past that?

"Let me call Ronin," I whispered, knowing I had no choice, even if the decision to do so was going to hurt us both. I could trust neither of them, but I believed Ronin had the power to stop my father. Made men were not restricted by something so common as laws or right and wrong. They were ruthless.

A heartbeat later, his grip loosened, and he took several steps away.

"I can't believe you just said that." His voice came out cold and quiet, which was at least half of how I felt inside.

"He's my fiancé," I reminded him, determined to see this through no matter what it took or cost me. "He knows how to handle my father."

"You do know how he *handles things*, right?"

I kept my face impassive, but I knew. Ronin killed people for a living. The details on his exploits were sketchy, but his reputation was strong enough to put the fear in anyone who considered crossing him. That might extend to Anthony Cullotta if Ronin was inclined to make it happen.

"He's my only chance."

FALLEN ANGEL

"Is that what you really believe?" His narrowed blue-green eyes turned glacial.

I hesitated.

"Alrighty then." He shook his head and backed away farther. "You don't want my help? Fine. I won't force you to do anything—for now. But don't say I didn't warn you."

I don't know why, but something about that outburst made me bite back a smile. He was acting like a petulant child who had his favorite toy stolen by the class bully. Of course, that made me the toy in that story and it didn't sit well at all.

"You think this is funny?"

I pressed my lips harder together for a few seconds more until I was sure I wouldn't break out in a fit of giggles. My fear had morphed me into an insecure teenager all over again. However, he was right, and there was nothing funny about this situation. Although maybe a bit of levity wouldn't hurt either.

"Not really, but it still feels weird having you here, trying to protect me from my own father. You might be overacting." I didn't think so, but it was still difficult to admit out loud that my asshole of a father cared so little for me that he would kill me over a handful of diamonds. I didn't want to believe it even though I knew it was true.

How exactly had things gotten to this point? And what did this mean for my sister? If he was actually planning to use her as leverage like he'd insinuated, then this whole situation was going to get really ugly and possibly bloody.

I really needed to talk to Ronin about my next step. Waiting for the legal system to do its thing was not a viable answer.

"Ronin Kavanaugh cannot be trusted. I might be the only one who is truly on your side in all of this."

Fresh anger rose again. "It's rather conceited of you to make that kind of assumption. And if that's truly the case, does that mean you are going to return the diamonds, so I can hand them over to my father in exchange for my life?"

"You know I can't."

And just like that, the door closed on the glimmer of hope I'd allowed inside.

One of these days, I would learn. The men in my life were never going to choose me first. I'd always come second, third or dead last. Whether it be money or power, or in this case, the law. If I was the kind of person who liked to discover what made people tick, it could be an intriguing case study. As it was, it was my life, and it was high time I figured my own shit out.

I tried to think of something clever to say, and couldn't. The anger deflated as resignation settled in. Still, I waited a moment more for him to say...anything. The silence stretched as we stared at each other, until I was ready to squirm.

"I've got to go," I finally said. "Everyone is waiting for me."

I braced for the fight, or at the very least, the sarcasm, which never came. Instead, he nodded, and stepped aside. I straightened my spine and walked to the door. I had to get out and get out quick. As I passed him, he finally spoke.

"Please be careful, Nova. I need you to stay alive."

* * *

HOURS LATER, after being put through what equated to a publicity gauntlet, I was ready to collapse. My feet ached in the four-inch heels I favored for public events, and I was pretty sure my facial muscles were going to ache tomorrow from all the smiling. Not that I wasn't thrilled with the turnout for our VIP pre-show. Thanks to my team, the hotel management, and Zia's amazing catering, everything had turned out perfectly. However, there were still two more days until the main event, and there were a lot of things that could go wrong.

I pinched the bridge of my nose to stave off the headache that had been building over the last hour, but it was when I tried to take a deep, relaxing breath and couldn't, I realized I had to actually take some action.

"You okay?" Trina leaned in and asked.

I nodded. "Yes. But with all this excitement, I need my inhaler."

"Where is it?" she asked, looking extremely concerned.

"Don't worry," I reassured her. "It's in my office backstage." For the last several weeks I'd operated out of a small makeshift office/dressing room while we prepared for the show. I normally kept my inhaler with me at all times, but wearing the form-fitting, short dress from my collection, I'd been forced to leave it behind.

"I'll get it and be right back."

I grabbed her wrist and stopped her. "Let me. I could use the five minutes to catch my breath and drink a glass of water. I'll be right back."

She nodded. "Okay, boss. We'll hold down the horde while you do what you need. Although with the amount of food and drink being served, I doubt anyone is going to notice you are gone. Everyone seems really happy with the party. But if you need anything, seriously, anything at all, just call me. My cell phone is hooked up to these damn things." she tapped the headset still firmly atop her head.

I laughed. "Okay. Thank you, I'm not sure what I would do without you."

"Me neither." She laughed as I left the group and made my way to my backstage office.

I still couldn't get that conversation with Rock out of my head. I needed to try and talk to him again and see if I could negotiate a deal with him about those diamonds. Knowing that my father was looking for me had shaken me and now I wasn't sure what my future held. If he thought I had his precious diamonds, he wasn't going to let that go. His and Luca's last visit now felt like a bad omen for something far worse and that creepy sensation of trouble coming crawled up my back.

I might have to take Rock up on protection after all. I'd lied to him and myself about my belief in Ronin. Ever since he'd questioned me about that night five years ago, I had a sinking feeling I was missing something important.

At my door, I entered the code, but so far I had not seen any of Ronin's supposedly beefed up security. Maybe they were so good they were present but unseen. It would be nice to get through the rest of the night without having to answer any more questions about the increased security. My bullshit story about a stalker had sounded reasonable enough when first asked, but it made me feel pretentious and petty.

Since I had not been lying about the inhaler, I reached for that first and took several puffs to calm the restriction I felt in my chest. I wasn't sure there was much worse than that feeling I got when I couldn't breathe. It was a weakness that could be debilitating if I wasn't prepared, and I hated it. But it was also a fact of life. So I refused to indulge in more than brief self-pity over it. I was about to take a seat at my desk when a knock sounded on the door behind me. My head snapped to the side at the same time a sigh left my lips.

I'd only needed five minutes alone to gather my thoughts and get my head back on straight. Was that too much to ask?

I opened the door to a man I didn't recognize, who wore a dark suit, a dark shirt and a scowl across his face. He looked like every other security guard Ronin had sent my way today. "Can I help you?"

When he didn't answer right away, I tried to close the door, but he shoved a foot in my way. I then tried to take a few steps back—also unsuccessful. The stranger grabbed me around the waist, pulled me close against him, and lifted his arm to my neck.

Before I could scream, I felt the prick at my skin, and the burning pain as something I was sure I didn't want was plunged into my neck. His other hand clamped across my mouth as I searched his face. Other than his heavy dark brows, crooked nose, and dark eyes there was nothing to give me even a clue who had sent him. But I knew.

I knew.

As my vision blurred and my limbs grew numb amidst the abject terror flooding through me, I realized my father had struck again.

And this time, I was on my own...

CHAPTER 8

Rock

Jesus Fucking Christ.

I'd watched that needle go into Nova's neck from across the room and couldn't move fast enough to stop it. My heart seized as she collapsed against the man who dared to hurt her. Panic and rage flooded through me as I ran for her.

Only seconds passed, but it could have been a lifetime. Thanks to all of the training and my time in the motorcycle club, I moved silently even at full speed. There was also a decent amount of noise coming from the rest of the backstage area to act as cover. He didn't see me coming. Not when I lunged for the door. Not when I grabbed the side of his head and slammed it into the door frame with a resounding crack— I didn't know whether it was the door or his head. I didn't care.

He crumpled immediately, his hold on Nova releasing. As she collapsed bonelessly, I dove for the floor beneath her to break her fall. I managed to grab her arm before it was too late, but our heads butted each other and pain exploded through my skull. I landed on the floor with her in my arms, and for a few seconds, I simply sat there in a daze before I could shake it off and pull her into my arms. I checked for a pulse, relieved it beat steady and strong beneath my fingers.

Thank God. Watching her get injected had nearly stopped my heart. If they had killed her... I shook my head again, forcing that image out of my mind. If I went there now, I wouldn't be able to think and right now she needed me to not only think, but do something to get her out of here.

I fished my cellphone out of my pocket and after unlocking the screen, pressed two numbers.

The man on the other end answered on the first ring. "What's wrong?"

"I need your help."

"Shit. Tell me."

"Backstage at the auditorium of The Sinclair. I have one man down and another injured. I'm going to need a path out of this hotel so we won't be seen. And a lot of fucking firepower to ensure we stay alive."

"Cullotta?"

"Yeah."

"Good. Now I don't need another excuse to mess that fucker up." He was right about that. I no longer cared about the letter of the law. Not with Nova in my arms, unable to move. Ten seconds—hell, *five* seconds—later, and they would have taken her and I might have never seen her again.

There was still one problem with JD and the club taking him down. It meant I couldn't make the fucker pay myself.

"We're fifteen minutes out. Do you think you can wait?"

"Probably not. Her preshow party just ended and we're going to be mobbed with press."

"Well, that fucks things up."

"Tell me something I don't know."

"I'll call your brother. See if he's closer."

I closed my eyes and silently cursed. I barely wanted to involve the MC, let alone Houston. When this op went sideways, and it would, I wanted to minimize how many people I put in the crosshairs.

But the clock was ticking, and I needed to get her out of here before someone came looking for their man. Speaking of...I turned to investigate his condition and immediately assessed it as *not good,* based on the pool of blood gathering under his head.

Fuck.

I didn't have time to get into the details of this once the guy was found. Hopefully, if I locked her door and told everyone she wasn't feeling well... Right, because Ronin was going to go along with that bullshit. Then there was the matter of the video surveillance in every inch of this hotel. I did need Houston to run point on that. He had a better relationship with The Sinclair manager and could likely hold him off.

"Okay, call him. But tell him I need him to run point with Gabe. I can get her out of here, but not without hitting camera surveillance."

"Can do, but don't worry about the cameras, Tel is already locked and loaded at his computer

FALLEN ANGEL

and can fix that shit. We'll meet you in the parking garage."

"I hope you're right." I disconnected the call, because there wasn't time for more talk. I lifted myself from the floor while steadying Nova in my arms. I'd seen her in all kinds of situations, but never so vulnerable. She looked as beautiful as ever, but I missed the fire in her eyes when she looked at me. Whether in lust or anger, it was always there. The idea that her father wanted to take that away from her angered me all over again. And where exactly was her supposed fiancé? I didn't need him in my way, but he needed his ass kicked for letting this happen on his watch.

Which was exactly why I'd refused to leave.

Reluctant to let her go, but knowing I couldn't just waltz out of here without telling her staff something, I placed her gently on the couch in the corner of the room. I brushed the hair out of her face and rubbed my finger across her lips. "Don't worry, baby. He'll only get to you over my dead body, and trust me, I'm not going anywhere."

I rushed out into the hall and clicked the door closed behind me just in time. A woman with a headset stood just on the other side, a confused expression planted on her pixie like face with matching spiked hair with purple on the ends. One of Nova's people I presumed.

"Uhm," she hesitated looking at me from her all of five-foot frame. I towered over her. "Where is Nova? The press is waiting for her."

"I'm afraid they will have to wait. Another day, perhaps." I hadn't meant to sound so harsh, but the circumstances had me on edge. Cullotta could send someone else back here any second and I didn't relish anyone else getting hurt tonight. There were too many people and too many possibilities.

"That's impossible." She tried to maneuver past me to Nova's door. "I'm sure Nova would agree."

"Nova is sick. She needs a doctor, not a room full of predatory press."

"What? Oh shit, I knew something was wrong. She told me—" When I moved to block her entry into Nova's dressing room, the little sprite froze, blinking up at me. "Who are you?"

The fact we'd kept all our time together a secret didn't do me any favors now. And it had become public knowledge that Nova had a fiancé, so I couldn't claim boyfriend status without raising some eyebrows. "A friend," I said, reaching into my jacket pocket where I kept my badge.

Her eyes widened as she followed the direction of my hand, relief sagging her face when she saw me pull out a wallet instead of what? A weapon? These people might be right to be cautious, but they were really paranoid, too. I flipped the folio open and showed her my badge. She grabbed a pen from her clipboard and proceeded to write down my information. Paranoid and efficient. I liked this woman and could see why Nova had hired her.

"Okay, Agent Reed. I don't know what the FBI has to do with this, but if Nova isn't able to attend the press conference, I've got to make alternate arrangements. But how bad is it? Should I call for an ambulance or a car to take her to the hospital?"

"Actually, a car would be perfect. I don't think she'd agree to an ambulance or emergency personnel running through the remnants of her party."

The woman nodded her head. "You're right about that. She could be at death's door and she'd probably kill me if I didn't do everything I could to keep this quiet."

Good girl.

E.M. GAYLE

"Sounds like you know exactly how to handle this," I said, turning back to Nova's office. If the assistant took care of the show as efficiently as I expected she would, then maybe Nova would be less likely to kill him when she woke. Considering what I was about to do, I highly doubted that. But that was a risk I was willing to take.

"Can you text me and let me know how she's doing?"

"I think she'll be fine."

"Still. I'd feel a lot better if I got confirmation after the doctor clears her."

I nodded.

"Perfect." She held out her hand, which I stared at without immediately understanding. "Give me your phone, and I'll add my contact info. My name's Trina by the way."

"Of course it is." I handed her my phone, she tapped the screen a bunch of times, and then handed it back. "There you go. All set. There should be a car waiting downstairs in the garage by the time you get there. I'd prefer if you took her through the back and away from the front entrance. Nova is a very private person and she won't want anything to end up in the press beyond whatever statement I make. Okay?"

She had no idea just how okay that was.

Nova's need to keep her private life under wraps worked into my plan perfectly. Maybe I wouldn't even need Houston to run interference for me with Gabe. Considering how much the manager seemed to dislike me, I kind of doubted that.

After Trina left to go and deal with the press, I wasted no time getting Nova the hell out of there. The longer it took, the more likely others would come looking for her. However, by the time we got to the garage entrance my nerves were shot.

How the hell did kidnappers get away so easily? This kind of work was stressful.

A black town car sat idling at the curb, the driver standing at the ready by the rear passenger door. When he saw me come through the revolving glass with Nova in my arms, he didn't bat an eye. "Agent Reed?" he asked.

"Yeah," I grunted as he rushed to open the door, and I placed her as gently as I could in the back seat.

"I'm afraid I'm going to have to terminate your services here." I said to the driver. "This is official business, and I can't take you with me."

"But, but—I can't leave the car," he stammered.

"Sure you can," a voice from the shadows

reassured him before stepping into the light. JD in his dark clothes, black leather cut, dark beard a few inches past needing a trim, and a swollen and bruised right eye emerged, looking every bit of death one would expect from him in a dark garage.

The fear from the driver as he looked between me and JD would have been laughable if they were under different circumstances. JD reached into his pocket and I thought the poor guy was going to piss his pants on the spot. To his obvious relief, JD pulled out his wallet and plucked out a handful of bills. "Go home early. We'll take this from here and I'll even make sure the car gets back to the agency before it's missed."

The guy didn't look like he believed him, but as the rest of the club roared into the parking garage and surrounded the car with their bikes, he must have decided no job was worth this kind of trouble. I would have agreed, except that my job led me into the shittiest places at the worst times, and I kept going back for more.

The driver took the generous donation JD was making to the cause, and headed into the hotel. "Keys are in the ignition," he called out just before he disappeared.

FALLEN ANGEL

"Just like old times," I stated with a frown. "Scaring the locals and assuming money will solve all of their problems."

"Money nearly always works. It's the international symbol for getting whatever the hell you want."

I rolled my eyes as I rounded the car. "I've got this from here."

"We'll escort you. I wouldn't put it past Cullotta to make a move. Which he might be less inclined to do if the club is with you."

I wanted to argue, but I didn't have time. I also had this undeniable need for no one to know where I planned on taking her. My apartment was one thing. I kept that on the down low, but it was the place I was willing to sacrifice. The other not so much.

"You can follow me to the city limits. After that I go the rest of the way on my own. I'll call you tomorrow and discuss what your hacker found out."

"Where are you going?"

I didn't answer. Instead, I slipped into the driver's seat and started the car. This wasn't a negotiation. Only time would tell if I'd done my job well enough to hide my refuge from his hacker.

99

E.M. GAYLE

I looked into the rear-view mirror at the woman in the backseat. She seemed to be sleeping peacefully, but I had a feeling when she woke there would be nothing peaceful at all. She was about to learn that I would do anything to protect what was mine.

Anything.

CHAPTER 9

Ronin

"Where is my fiancée?"

JD Monroe glanced up and looked at me as if I was a fucking piece of gum on his shoe. "Why would I know where *your* fiancée is? I don't fucking know you."

I seethed. When I wanted answers, I expected answers. "Because she is with *your* son." I wasn't sure how I felt about the fact that I'd learned that Rock Reed had grown up within a motorcycle club that had dealt in nearly every illegal operation you could imagine.

"Ahh" He leaned forward and placed his

E.M. GAYLE

elbows on the table, steepling his fingers in front of his face. "You must be Kavanaugh. I believe my son may have mentioned you."

"Well, that's great, but I'm not here to have fucking tea. My fiancée was last seen with Agent Reed giving out some bullshit story about taking her to the hospital because she was sick. Now, they are nowhere to be found."

Monroe lifted his shoulders. "Are you calling my son a liar?"

I sighed, and then took a deep breath. There wasn't time to add a new player to the game.

I could only imagine the depth his father's life added to Reed's job as a Federal Agent. The extra layers made him a slightly more interesting opponent for sure. However, I would still win. Nothing less would be acceptable.

"I could attribute your son with many labels and it wouldn't matter. He has taken what belongs to me, and I expect her to be returned to me immediately."

Monroe leaned back in his chair, crossing both his arms and his legs. "Last I checked, this was still a free country. We don't own women anymore. Or did your family not get the memo?"

"Oh, an enlightened motorcycle club president. Just what the world needs." His amusement at my expense went beyond annoying. I crossed my arms over my chest. "My family is none of your business. At least, not yet. However, if I do not get what I want immediately, then this situation could escalate from a nuisance to conflict. I highly doubt you want to go there."

"Is that some sort of threat? You should probably know that I don't take those well." He clenched his meaty hands into fists and I imagined all the barbaric ways someone like him might use them, none of which phased me in the least.

"It's simply facts. You give me what I want and tell me where I can find Agent Reed, and we can both get back to our respective business." Although I couldn't help but wonder what business brought the entire motorcycle club so far from home. I highly doubted it was a simple family visit. A father and son reunion did not need an entire club to happen.

Not to mention the fresh wounds on Monroe's face and arms. And the stitches on his arm looked homegrown versus hospital grade. A clear indicator that his injuries were the kind he didn't want to report. I made a mental note that after this meeting I would get my team to investigate. If there was more to be discovered, I needed that information sooner rather than later.

"Sounds like you need to mind your own house more than mine. If your fiancée prefers the company of my son more than yours, then you have a much bigger problem than your current lack of information."

I clenched my teeth and felt the strong pulse of the muscle in my cheekbone that ticced with every heartbeat. I could see that Monroe intended to antagonize me, much like his son.

I took the empty seat across from him. The big biker in his leather vest covered with patches, black button-down shirt, and worn in jeans was about as out of place as possible in a hotel such as this. And yet, the air of confidence and fuck off expression on his face made him fit in more than he should.

"Look, our families have no business together, but we also have no quarrel—for now. But this situation is riding a line that I don't believe you are interested in crossing."

He leaned forward and retrieved a cigar from the case that sat in front of him. "You'd be surprised what I might be interested in. Take this cigar, for instance. Someone with only half a brain would look at me and probably assume I'd have no interest in or be capable of indulging in something this expensive or this frivolous. They'd be wrong, of course, considering this is my second case of these this month." He pulled out a silver engraved lighter and lit the cigar, closing his eyes and savoring the scent and the taste. "My point is, if you're going to make assumptions about people, take the time to look past the surface. You and I? We aren't as different as you might think."

I couldn't be further from the MC president if I tried. However, I was curious to hear what else he had to say. "How so?" I asked.

"We are both driven by family." he pointed out. "Yours more blood than all of mine. But family is not blood relation for everyone. Rockford is my blood, but he's not the only family I have. My entire club is my family. Honor is strong among my men, as is loyalty. It's the lifeblood for families like ours. Without it we are nothing."

I signaled for the waiter as I let his words sink in. I had no plans to concede his point, even if some of what he said made sense. Our family lived like royalty amongst the richest men in the world. We did not simply occupy a small corner of the Pacific Northwest. We ruled entire cities.

E.M. GAYLE

"I know what you're thinking."

"I doubt that," I said, taking the glass of scotch the waiter had returned with. "The assumptions you make about me could be just as wrong as the ones I've made about you."

A bark of laughter burst from the older man. "Well, hell. I guess you are right about that. I guess all that really matters is that we are going to have to agree that we don't like each other very much and move on."

"I can get behind that."

Monroe continued to suck on his cigar as I savored the twenty-three-year-old scotch that went down as smooth as melted butter with a little bite at the back end.

"I'm not going to tell you where he is because I honestly don't know. But you need to know that even if I did, I wouldn't tell you. On paper, my son and I may not seem to get along all that well, what with him being a federal agent and all, but he is still my son. Nothing will ever break that bond."

I mulled over his words. I believed he was telling me the truth. Whether he knew or not mattered little to him, but it meant everything to me. If the son had not divulged his location to his father, then he was taking all the precautions necessary to keep Nova safe.

This gave me the time I needed to get further under Cullotta's skin without any interference or concern for Nova's involvement, at least until the moment was right. It was time to get to the bottom of my grandfather's death. JD was right about one thing. Honor was everything, and my grandfather's murderer had to deal with the consequences.

"You're remarkably calm for a man whose fiancée is missing. Is there another reason you are here?"

"Nothing that would concern you. I've done my homework, and I know what kind of club you run. On one hand I can commend you for your intriguing brand of vigilante justice—I am very much an eye-for-an-eye type of man. On the other, I can see that our business interests would not exactly align unless you chose to return to your roots in which case I'd be interested. However, in this case, it's better for all involved if you and your club sit this one out. Agent Reed has already overstepped his bounds, you don't want to compound that issue by getting involved."

"While you've done your due diligence, I'll

give you that, you clearly didn't get the message. We don't take threats well, even veiled ones. If you don't want us in your business, then you should take it elsewhere. Vegas is not your territory." He snubbed the burning end of his cigar down in the dish in front of him. "I also don't appreciate that you're ruining the taste of my cigar with your bullshit."

Okay then, we were putting the false pleasantries aside. I could live with that. His insults meant nothing to me. "Don't get your panties in a twist biker. I have more than enough on my agenda for this trip, which will be over soon." I drained the remainder of my scotch and stood up. "Stay out of my way, and we won't have to see each other again."

I knew my warning fell on deaf ears, but this meeting would get back to his son and if nothing else it would rile up the boy scout into making a move. Me and Nova, we weren't done. Not until I was satisfied my mission was complete.

All of it.

CHAPTER 10

Nova

"How big of a problem is it?"

The sound of Rock's voice in the distance roused me. I tried to orient myself as to what was happening. I rubbed at my eyes that felt gritty and heavy, which were the hallmarks of an extended amount of sleep. I ran my fingers through my hair. That's when I felt the twinge in my neck. My hand snapped to the sore spot and I remembered the stranger standing in my door, sticking something in that exact spot.

That was all I could remember. The panic that rose now resembled the fear I felt then at the lingering sensation of losing control. My vision had blurred, the room had spun, a loud, sharp noise had filled the small space a moment before my legs gave out and I fell. Seeing and feeling it happen in slow motion had been surreal and even now, goosebumps pricked at my skin.

My eyes snapped open as I jerked forward to a sitting position. Where the hell was I?

I glanced around the room, searching for familiar details that would tell me something —anything.

"I've got to go. She's awake."

Rock's voice again. Where? Was I dreaming?

"Finally. You're awake. How do you feel?"

One second I was alone in an unfamiliar place, and the next the man of my dreams was kneeling in front of me, his eyes filled with concern.

"Where am I? What happened? What the hell is going on?" My voice rose to near hysteria by the third question, matching the panic flooding through me.

"Easy now. One question at a time, and then we'll go from there, okay?" He reached forward and touched my face, his fingers tracing a pattern down my cheek and along my jawline.

Something wasn't right. I swatted his hand away. "Don't touch me. Answer my questions."

He didn't smile or laugh. Instead, his expression remained neutral, and that unnerved me more than any other reaction he could have had. Frustrated, I bared my teeth. "Please. Just answer the questions."

He stood and crossed the room, only returning after he'd retrieved a bottle of water. "Drink. And since you said please..."

I swiped the bottle from his hand and took a drink only because my throat was so dry, it hurt to talk. Although I still glared at him as I drank half the bottle. I felt marginally better.

"You're at my place," he started. "I brought you here because you need somewhere safe to hide, and no one except me knows it exists. Out here, we won't have to worry about someone coming to look for you."

My brows raised, and I didn't know whether that statement was meant to reassure me or scare the hell out of me. In front of the couch there were large sliding doors that went from the floor to the ceiling, and if I wasn't wrong, they looked like the kind that would slide completely out of the way and leave the room completely open to the outdoors. More importantly, I could see the landscape beyond his back deck and pool area and it wasn't the desert of Las Vegas. In fact, it was the complete opposite of the desert. There were lots of big trees, green rolling hills, and snowcapped mountains off into the distance.

"Okay. But where is it? That," I pointed out the window, "does not look like Vegas."

"Because it's not. While I do have an apartment in town, it's not as hidden as this place. Taking you there would have made you a sitting duck."

"A sitting duck for who?" I asked, even though I was pretty sure I knew the answer.

He ignored that question and instead continued with my previous questions. "As for what happened..." He hesitated, running his hands through his hair. "I caught someone shoving a needle into your neck."

"With what?"

"That's impossible to know without a blood test. There are quite a few drugs on the market capable of knocking someone out in under a minute."

"Great. That's reassuring."

"I wasn't trying to reassure you. I warned you that you weren't safe, and you chose to ignore me. Whatever it was, he disabled you within seconds, and if I had not happened to have been there, you would not be here.

"Where would I have been?" I needed some kind of confirmation that my father had tried to have me kidnapped.

"You tell me. I'm not privy to where your father takes his victims to torture them, but if you'd like to share that information it could be extremely useful in my future endeavors."

"Neither am I. My father cut me off from all contact until recently. He wanted me nowhere near anything to do with my family, him, or his organization. So, this whole ruse you've had going since you met me has been a colossal waste of both of our time. I know nothing."

"Except somehow you had the one thing he wanted the most. Those diamonds were worth a fortune."

He didn't know the half of it. My father had a plan for those diamonds that had more to do with power than they did money. He would trade them for information and position—

"Wait. Did you say they *were* worth a fortune? What does that mean?"

His face darkened, and I could now see the anger he'd been trying to hide.

I looked around the spacious but cozy cabin.

E.M. GAYLE

The dark, masculine colors of the room spoke of comfort and power without a need for bells and whistles. There was lots of leather, wood, and glass with very little light other than the natural light from the generous windows. On the one hand, it made you want to settle in for some quiet, cozy solitude, and on the other, it screamed with the fact that here, in the middle of the woods, you were alone and on your own. There were no neighbors, or passersby to remind you that you were no longer in a crowded city with anything you could want at your fingertips.

"We need to go." I swung my feet off the couch and stood, ignoring the lightheaded feeling that nearly knocked me back down. "I'm not supposed to be here."

"I think you are right where you need to be." He stalked closer, and that unsettled feeling intensified. "It's the perfect place to get some answers from you."

I tried to take a step back, only to be reminded that I was trapped against a piece of furniture, with no real way to escape. What the hell was wrong with me? Why, after all the intimate nights with this man when I didn't know his name, did I suddenly feel frightened now?

This man had commanded my body in ways that no one else would have dared. And I'd not only allowed it, I'd reveled in it. Every command, whether spoken or unspoken had propelled me to a place that freed me from previous constraint.

Not now. This was different. He was different.

"What about the VIP party? I was supposed to meet with the press. Trina must be going out of her mind. My friends too. They will be searching everywhere."

He shook his head. "Nope. They all think you had an asthma attack and I rushed you to the hospital for treatment. They are worried, yes. But they're not looking for you."

"Jesus Christ, Rock. Are you trying to ruin my career?"

"If that is your biggest concern right now, then your priorities are seriously fucked up. I'm trying to keep you alive."

"By what? Hiding me? That's not going to work. I can't stay here forever."

"I don't need forever."

"Then how long? How long to you expect me to stay here?"

"As long as it takes."

I was ready to throw my hands in the air. Frustration rolled over me like a freight train. "For what? I need to go back today. Not just to salvage the press conference, but to talk to my father. This isn't just about me."

"You're not going back and that's final. Not until I think it's safe."

My mouth dropped open at the finality of his words.

"Have you lost your mind?" Probably not the best choice of words considering the circumstances. I was having trouble staying calm.

He shrugged. "Maybe. It's impossible for me to be impartial when it comes to your safety. I'll do whatever it takes to keep you alive, including piss you off."

I was so angry right now I could spit. And yet, his conviction and goal were not unreasonable. They both were actually kind of hot if I really thought about it. I shook my head to stop that line of thinking. I could *not* condone his methodology.

"I'm not kidding around with you, Rock. You cannot keep me here against my will."

"Actually, I can if I want, and there's not much you could do to stop me."

I sputtered.

"Do you think you could find your way out of here and back to Vegas without me? We may only be hours away from your destination, but I guarantee just getting past these woods would be too much to handle on your own."

Was that supposed to be some sort of threat? Or scare tactic? "You're being an asshole," I finally said as my mind began to settle on just how precarious a position he had put me in.

"I'd rather be an asshole in a world where you lived than a nice guy who had to live a life without you in it."

Well, shit. Every time he thumped his chest and declared I couldn't survive without him, he went and said something like that. How was I even supposed to take that? I had no defense against those kinds of words.

Except there was still the matter of my sister.

"You don't understand. Nothing about this situation is that cut and dry or simple."

"You got that right."

I ignored that dig and continued. "This isn't just about me."

"Don't do that again, Nova. I don't give a shit about your fiancé or whatever agreement he made with your father. The second your father decided your life was forfeit, everything changed. You aren't going to marry that asshole. I won't allow it. If I have to tie your ass to a chair and keep you here until both those fuckers are in jail, that's what I'm going to do."

A deep sigh worked its way from my throat. I collapsed back onto the sofa, feeling the weight of the world settle around my shoulders. I'd dug myself a hole at age eighteen, and it seemed five years later, it had only gotten deeper. I was no closer to getting out of it than I had been back then.

"Please, Rock. You need to listen to me. I wasn't talking about Ronin. I never wanted to marry him. Nearly every single thing I've done over the last five years was so that I could get out of that scenario. Only, it seems no matter how hard I try, I can't break free. You know I took the diamonds, and you know why. What you don't really know is how."

"That's pretty evident at this point. You stole them. And there's a video tape that proves it. It's a moot point."

I shook my head, unable to deny I'd screwed that part up pretty bad. "You're not asking the right questions, Agent Reed. It's not about how I actually got my hands on them, it's how I found out about them in the first place."

"I don't see how that really matters, either. Not unless you are going to admit that you are more a part of your father's organization than you keep insisting on." He tapped his fingers on his leg. "Although, now that I think about it, I would like to know. Are you going to tell me, or do I have to guess?"

I'd never in a million years planned to betray my sister's involvement. But if it convinced him I couldn't stay away from Vegas for a second longer it would be worth it. The longer I hid from my father, the greater chance he took things out on her.

"If I tell you, will you promise me that we can go back to the city as soon as possible?"

"No." His answer came so quick and blunt it felt like a slap to my face.

"Please, Rock. What do I have to do to convince you? You and I can take the diamonds back to the city, arrange a trade with my father, and then I can help you catch my father redhanded with those diamonds if you let me. Wouldn't that work? We can both get what we want if we work together."

"What kind of scam are you trying to run here, Nova? You and I both know I don't have 'the diamonds.'

His use of air quotes around the diamonds confused me. What was he trying to say? His anger at me made no sense. What the heck was I missing?

He shoved his hands in his pockets and stalked across the room away from me. "I haven't figured out what kind of con you are trying to run on me, but I will. And until then, we are not going anywhere. You can beg, cajole, and plead however much you want. I'm not changing my mind. Not until you tell me the god damned truth."

"Truth about what? About my sister? Or the fact that my father has imprisoned her and threatened her life if I don't toe the line? Is that what you wanted to hear?"

He turned slowly to me, his face still impassive as before. "No. But I know the fucking truth. And until you start talking, we're going exactly nowhere."

Her head was definitely going to explode. "What truth?! What are you talking about?"

He walked over to stand in front of me and reached down to grab my chin.

"The diamonds, Nova. I know they're not real."

CHAPTER 11

Rock

This woman infuriated me to no end. Her inability to just be honest was enough to drive me mad. I didn't care if that was a case of kettle meet pot. I'd had no choice but to keep my identity from her. But this? This was malicious.

"What do you mean the diamonds aren't real?" The hysteria in her voice annoyed him. He didn't need her theatrics any more than he needed her lies. He was tired, hungry, and contending with the fact that despite everything, he couldn't stop thinking about fucking her. The inappropriateness of that fact didn't seem to matter. At least not to his dick.

"Enough, Nova." He released her chin and walked away from her again. Every time he touched her, his mind splintered between duty and need. "The charade is over."

"Fuck you, Agent Reed. I'm not trying to play some game with you."

He closed his eyes against her curse. Her anger should have helped his case not hinder it. It should have been enough to give him the perspective he desperately needed to get out of his own head. And yet, whether she angrily called him Agent Reed or softly called him Rock, it had the same affect.

"I don't understand how you thought giving me fakes would work. You had to know it was only a matter of time before I figured it out. Were you trying to buy some time? Did you already give them to your father, and now that he doesn't need you, he wants to kill you?" He turned back to her. "Say something, dammit."

She stood from the couch, straightening her back and arching her neck like a queen about to dress down someone beneath her. And fuck if she didn't look beautiful like that.

"I did not give you fake diamonds. That's

FALLEN ANGEL

ridiculous. Each one of them were inspected and authenticated by someone I trust."

He wanted to meet this person she trusted, because he found it hard to believe she trusted anyone at all. And if she did, why?

"Our forensics lab isn't going to give me anything other than the black and white facts, and the facts are, they are not real. So, there is a definite disconnect somewhere. Either you're lying or I'm lying, or someone else is involved I'm not aware of. Either way, I'd say we're both fucked, and not in the good way that I can't stop thinking about."

She sucked in a breath at his confession. "Don't do that."

"What? Be honest? Sweetheart, as far as I can tell that's all we have left. Either we are honest with each other or we're both dead."

"Then don't accuse me of a crime in one breath and tell me you want to fuck me in the next."

I crossed back to her and pulled her tight against me. I had expected a fight, and while she did stiffen, she also didn't try to get away. "Keep talking like that, and I won't be responsible for what happens next. For every filthy word that comes out of your mouth, I'd like to bend you

123

E.M. GAYLE

over and spank your ass. Seriously. Now is not the time to push."

"You wouldn't dare," she hissed, her eyes going wide.

Laughter bubbled up. "You have no idea what I'm capable of. But before this case is over, you will."

"And that's the problem right there," she spat, recovering quickly. "I'm nothing but a case. Always have been, always will."

I reached up and wrapped a hand around her neck. Not to hurt her so much as to restrain her, although I couldn't lie that the little flash of fear I saw, before it got replaced with anger, made my dick get just a little bit harder. Something I thought was impossible at this point.

There was something about her that pushed at every button I possessed. Where I normally held my control in a tight, ruthless grip, with her, my ability to stand fast unraveled. Every time I turned around, I found myself in a state of reaction instead of proaction. It had been a damn joke to think that mixing business with my pleasure wouldn't burn me in the end. Yet, I hadn't seen her coming. I'd lost my edge. And now I had to rewrite the rules between right and wrong, and good and bad. I had crossed a line

124

that was bound to leave a permanent mark for us both.

Now I had a decision to make. Either she would be my weakness, and thus my downfall, or I would reshape my path, and hers, into something entirely new. Where crossing a line no longer mattered...

"Do you have any idea how much easier all of this would be if you meant nothing to me? If I could just walk away and never have to worry about the fallout, I could run this op, nail your father to the wall, and take out his business partners in one fell swoop. Hell, I could round you up as well. It won't be long until we have a copy of the videotape your father procured. It would be all the evidence I need to add your name to the list. Being in possession of blood diamonds is a serious offense." I ground my teeth across every syllable, uncaring if I made her mad. She wanted the truth and that's what she was going to get. "I wasn't supposed to get attached."

I leaned forward, placing my face at her neck and breathed deep. There wasn't a thing about her I didn't miss when I left her after each of our encounters. But her scent, it did something crazy to my brain, and I couldn't get enough of it. If I was a smart man, I'd bottle that shit up and sell it like perfume and then make a million fucking dollars. Except then I'd have to share her, and I'd learned in the last week that I would never share anything about her.

She was mine.

She would marry another man over my dead body.

I crashed my mouth onto hers and took the kiss I was dying for. And she kissed me back. All tongues, teeth, and desperation as we tangled together mercilessly. To my delight, she gave as good as she got. I fished my hands through her hair and pulled, and she returned that pain in kind. My scalp burned, and I fucking loved it.

We were both angry with each other and turned on and desperate. It was a heady combination that I couldn't get enough of, and this kiss was the match to start the fire that would burn us both alive.

I leaned my weight against her, enough to make her lose her balance and topple back onto the couch. I followed her down. I half expected her nails to scrape down my face or her hands to push against my chest. Anything that might stop this before it went too far. But it didn't happen. She grabbed my head instead and held me tighter against her as we both frantically deepened the kiss.

Before I completely lost my mind, I tore my mouth from hers. "No more lies?"

She nodded. "Definitely. I hate not being able to tell the truth."

I wasn't sure I believed her, but I was too far gone to let that stop me. As if she sensed what I needed, she surged her hips forward, putting additional pressure I didn't need against my dick. "Fuck," I groaned, biting at her lip and reaching for her breast so I could tease a nipple. "You are impossible to resist. I can't stay away from you."

"Is that what you want? To stay away?" Her words were breathless and hot against my neck.

"Fuck no. Although you do make me feel things I shouldn't. I need to protect you. I want to keep you here and hidden from the world so you are safe. Is that so difficult to comprehend? I'm not sure what I would do if anything happened to you, but I am pretty sure the world doesn't want to know."

My words must have spurred her on, as she grabbed my shirt and shoved it up to my neck and her nails scratched a deep path down my back. I ground down, making sure my dick pressed against her clit.

"I won't be held like a prisoner," she panted, holding me tighter. "You have to understand that I can never live like that again. You have to take me back."

Her words angered me further. Or maybe it was the fact of how stubborn she continued to be. I didn't want to go against her wishes, but if anything happened to her...

Fuck. I couldn't wait any longer. The desire to dominate her the only way she would allow burned through my brain. I needed to be inside of her right now. Reaching between us, I lifted her dress and shoved her panties out of my way until I could feel the wet heat between her legs that told me so much more than her words ever would. She wanted me. She loved it when I took control. I slipped a finger between the lips of her sex and toyed with her clit until she squirmed and writhed against me.

"There you are, princess. Show me how much you want it." My words were short and hard as I grappled to stay in control.

"You're driving me crazy. You make me want to scream and come."

A bitter, tight laugh escaped my throat. The knowledge that her mind was as twisted as mine

FALLEN ANGEL

burrowed deep into my heart where it would never get out. I had to take her.

"Tell me you're ready." I thrust two fingers inside her before she could answer.

"Rock!" She jackknifed forward as much as my body would allow. Her nails scored deeper into my flesh.

"Tell me you're mine," I growled, barely hanging on.

"Yes. I'm yours," she cried out as my thumb pressed down on her clit.

"Tell me you'll do what I say to keep you safe." I angled my fingers upward and rubbed against the sensitive spot that all but guaranteed she'd come on command.

"Don't make me make a promise I can't keep."

Crushing disappointment pressed down on me. Although I wasn't sure whether it was her or me that caused it. I should have withdrawn. Stopped her from having an orgasm. Denial would have been a proper punishment at this point. But I was weak. To deny her pleasure, would deny it for both of us. Nothing made me happier than watching her fall apart when I ordered her to come.

"Then come, little liar. Come." I ruthlessly stroked in and out of her until she did exactly as

I ordered. Her legs shook so hard, I was pretty sure her bones rattled. As much as I wanted to be inside her so I could feel her tight muscles clamp around me, this right here did me in more. She threw her head back and screamed, her lips quivering as much as her pussy.

Fucking A. I loved her so much it hurt. She wasn't going to let me wrap her up in bubble wrap and keep her safe. I'd have to take her back to Vegas and watch her walk into harm's way, and it was going to kill me.

After she collapsed back into the couch, I lost track of how much time passed with the scent and heat of her permeating every inch of me. I stroked her pussy until the last of her aftershocks faded away, and still, I couldn't get enough. My dick strained to get my attention, but I ignored it. I didn't want to just fuck anymore. I wanted to love.

I just wasn't sure how.

"That's exactly what I was talking about," she whispered, finally breaking the peaceful silence enveloping us. "You can't be an asshole in one breath and nice in the next. You're giving me whiplash."

"Welcome to the club, Nova. Welcome to the club."

CHAPTER 12

Nova

"This is quite some place you have here." I'd heard the glass door open and close, and while he'd yet to say anything, I could feel him standing behind me waiting for something.

"It reminds me of home."

"Homesick?"

"Not exactly. I did love Washington State though. The cool air, the trees, the mist nine months out of the year."

"You're not going to find rain like that in sunny California."

A soft chuckle sounded behind me and the vibration of it hummed through my entire body. It gave me a three second look into what a normal life with someone like Rock Reed could be like. It made me long for something I shouldn't.

"What makes you think that's where we are? You slept through most of the trip."

"Common sense, and a halfway decent geography teacher in high school. Plus, Big Bear was one of my brother's favorite vacation spots. We spent a lot of time here during the unbearable heat of the Vegas summers."

He came forward and sat, stretching his big body on the lounge chair beside mine.

"I can't picture your family doing the cabin at a lake vacation thing. Honestly, I can't picture Anthony doing anything but work."

I snorted. "He is a workaholic. Doesn't have much time for family. But he had no problem sending his family away on vacations when he needed a break from having all of us underfoot. Having us around got on his nerves. It made me question why he insisted on having so many kids. He seemed to hate most of us."

"Parents do strange things we may never understand. It's impossible to know what went on in their minds back then." That sounded like maybe Rock was talking about his own family rather than mine. "What about you?" he asked. "Did you enjoy Big Bear?"

I shrugged. "It was okay. I kept to myself a lot back then. My brothers were obnoxious little assholes as pre-teens and my sister was too young to do anything with. But I had my art. I sketched everything back then, not just clothing. After a few days of drawing mountains and trees, I missed home and the city. The country is a nice escape, but I like the energy of Vegas. There's always more color—more life—in a place like that. Even the seedier side of life there draws my attention." I whipped my head to the side and met his gaze. "Have you ever been to Amsterdam?"

He shook his head. "I can count the number of places I've been on both my hands, and they don't include many international hotspots."

"It's got a similar vibe to Vegas, but with a richer history that seems to make everything seem brighter and more exciting. I thought about moving there after New York, but I missed home, so I came back here instead."

"That's another thing that surprises me.

Anthony gave you a lot of freedom. Isn't that unusual in families like yours?"

I stiffened. I'd managed to open Pandora's box without even realize I was doing it. I'd have to tread carefully until it closed again. "Families like mine..." I sighed. "I guess you could say that. As you know, marriages for the women are often arranged, and it's not out of the norm for it to happen at a young age."

"You don't have to sidestep around the truth, Nova. My job is to understand the mafia from the inside out and that includes the cultural norms, families behaviors as well as any legal and illegal businesses that are run. We probably know these men and their families better than their own mothers. Your own parents' marriage was arranged when your mother was just seventeen."

He was right. I should have known he would know more about the inner workings of my own family than I did. So, what was he trying to get at? "Are you interrogating me then? Is there some information about my father you are hoping to gain from this line of questioning?" I hated sounding so defensive, but I didn't know what to think. My emotions were a little on the raw side.

"No, I am not trying to interrogate you. I

want to know *you,* the woman. It just so happens that what I know about your family contradicts your experience. I thought that might be something you'd want to share. If I've hit a sore spot in your family history, I'm sorry. Consider my question taken back."

A deeper sigh pushed through my lips. I was being defensive because he was right, there were things that I needed to share with him. I just wasn't ready to go there yet. "I'm sorry," I said quietly. "I'm overly sensitive when it comes to Anthony. Our relationship is complicated and talking about him is painful. I'm still having trouble with the fact that my own father might hurt me or worse over those diamonds. And now I can't even give them to him in the hopes of getting him off my back. All I've ever really wanted was for him to let me live the life I want, not the life he expects."

"It's a tall order for a man like him. He has his priorities in all the wrong places, and he's too stubborn to realize it."

My heart squeezed and my throat went dry. Of course he was right. Although stubborn might be too nice of a word. However, I appreciated that Rock would soften his thoughts toward a criminal he hated just for my sake.

E.M. GAYLE

"Were you thinking about a swim?" He asked, abruptly changing the subject.

"Do I have time?"

"Time before what?"

"Before we go back," I said, alternately pointing and flexing my toes as I soaked in the warmth of the sun on my fair skin. I couldn't risk staying out here much longer if I didn't want to burn. "I still have a lot to do before the show."

"I haven't decided what our next move should be. My team has been unable to locate your father."

"And Ronin?"

"You still want to know where he is, after everything?" The surge of anger in his tone almost made me smile. Jealousy wasn't normally an attractive trait, but there was something special about Rock Reed that made possessiveness look exceptionally good on him.

"I'm asking if Ronin knows where my father is. He must be looking for me by now and he'll likely look there first. I could call him and speak with him. Pave the way, so to say."

He looked at me and shook his head. Clearly, he did not think that was a good idea.

"Nova, I don't need you to pave my way with Ronin. I can handle him on my own."

I didn't exactly doubt that, but men like Ronin and my father didn't play by the same rules someone like Rock did. They broke the rules and the law at their whim. He didn't have that luxury.

"I'm just offering up ideas. I know you have a job to do, but so do I. I want to be smart about it, but we have to come up with whatever it takes to get me back there. I won't miss that show. Not for any reason."

I half expected him to refuse to get me back in time. What he didn't know was that I was prepared to fight him on every front. I knew perfectly well that fashion sounded frivolous to most, but this moment—this show—if I didn't find a way out of marrying Ronin-it might be the best I ever have.

"Aren't you worried about your father? He isn't the kind of criminal you toy with. I've got more files on people he's had killed than people he still does business with."

I cringed, knowing he was right. My father had turned into a monster. Only what Rock didn't know…. "Isn't that what you are doing?"

He shrugged. "That's my job. I believe I stand in a slightly safer position than you do. There's a lot less chance he will try to kill me."

I shuddered. He might be right, but I trusted Anthony Cullotta about as far as I could throw him. He had sent me out into the world alone long before I was ready and I'd had to steal, scrape, and lie to get by for a long time.

But that was nothing compared to what I'd done that night. Another shiver worked down my spine. As much as I tried to forget, it never seemed to quite go away. It gave my father powerful leverage over me and he damned well knew it.

"Tell me what's really going on? Are you and Ronin planning something?"

I snapped my head to the side to look at him. That would certainly be interesting, if we were. I was having a hard time seeing a new path out of the trouble threatening to drown me. Ronin still seemed like my best shot. As his wife, there would be an opportunity to ask for help and an expectation to receive it. I let out the breath I'd caught and held.

Of course, that would mean that Ronin would have to be willing to help anyone but himself and that seemed unlikely. "No. Ronin is every inch the lone wolf he appears to be. I made zero progress in convincing him to work with me against my father."

"No. I don't imagine he would. Ronin is different. I'm having a hard time understanding what he really wants from me and he doesn't share anything from what I can tell."

"He's a game player. A risk-taker, if you will. He doesn't always have a clear-cut motive, beyond he likes to play, and he likes to win even more. Which makes your fiancé even more dangerous than your father."

"I guess you have a big folder of information on him too."

"Some. Although not nearly as much as I'd like. As a resident of the state of New York, he's a little bit out of my jurisdiction. However, the New York office is curious about his extended stay in Vegas and has shared some files with us. I'm also working another angle that might tell me more."

"Why are you telling me all of this? Isn't there some sort of law enforcement code where your case information is supposed to be secret?"

He laughed again, and I reveled in the delicious sound that vibrated through me. Seriously, if I could record that and sell it, I was pretty sure I would make a fortune because women around the world would go nuts for it.

"I haven't told you anything confidential. I

think it's safe to assume I'm going to have information on all the players that could touch my case. It's part of the job."

"Including me." It wasn't a question or a statement, so much as a realization for me. And a reminder that I was part of his case. It's how this whole thing had gotten started.

"Is this kind of fraternization between an agent and a person involved in his case allowed?"

For a long time he didn't answer. We both sat silently staring out over the pool. I'd obviously hit a nerve. But if it was going to be an elephant in the room, it should probably be addressed. How else would we move past it?

Maybe I would take that swim. Although I didn't exactly come prepared."How far away are your neighbors?" I asked.

He nearly choked. "Excuse me? What in the world does that have to do with anything."

"I figured if we weren't going to talk anymore, maybe I would go for that swim. But I don't have a suit to wear, so if I'm going to go naked, I should probably know ahead of time if I'm going to scandalize any of your neighbors."

"We're in the middle of a fifteen-acre property. Unless someone is watching with a telescope, they aren't likely to notice." I could hear the amusement in his voice and again, I enjoyed the fact I could make him smile. Both our worlds were a jumbled mess of horrible people, wanting us to focus on more evil than two people should suffer. We definitely needed the levity.

"Okay," I said as I stood and dropped the robe I'd found in his bathroom. When I took a step towards the pool, his hand snaked out and wrapped around my bare thigh.

"Honestly, I shouldn't have gotten involved with you. It's a rookie mistake, and I definitely know better. But watching you in that hotel bar... there was something about you that I couldn't resist. And just so we're one hundred percent clear, it wasn't the desire to get information from you that got me to break protocol."

I could barely breathe as he spoke. The warmth between my thighs from his presence traveled up and through my body, wrapping around my heart. There seemed nothing I could do to stop it. Yes, I'd fallen hard and fast for him, but that didn't diminish my feelings. It did, however, put us both in more danger. I wasn't supposed to fall in love with a man I couldn't stay with.

"Do you regret it?"

Shit. I never meant for that question to slip

out. It sounded so pathetic to ask something like that. Of course he regretted it. Being with me compromised his job. But he would never admit to me. That's not the kind of man he was.

"Absolutely not."

I closed my eyes, willing the burn of tears to recede. I wanted to believe so badly I ached with it.

"Nova, look at me."

I shook my head, afraid to do as he demanded. I was going to cry, and my only escape was the pool. I pulled free from him and rushed to the side and dove in before I could change my mind or he stopped me. Underneath the water, a sob tore through me, and for a few seconds, I let it happen. I had to get it out before I started screaming bloody murder.

My moment of solitude was broken when he dove into the water next to me. I jerked when he circled me in his arms, but went limp when he pulled us both to the surface.

He slicked back my hair from my face and used his finger underneath my chin to force me to look at him. "I know you don't think you can believe what I say. But you must. I refuse to believe that what we have is tainted forever by

FALLEN ANGEL

how it started. I didn't think I could tell you the truth then, but now I know it was a mistake."

"We both made mistakes. I'm not mad anymore. I just—"

"Tell me."

"We can't stay together," I sobbed. "My father will never allow it. He can and will hurt me, that's inevitable. But if he comes after you because of me…? I—I just can't."

He wiped my face, taking away the tears I wasn't even aware were falling. "Shhh," he crooned. "This isn't your job, it's mine."

I blinked, looking up at him. "What does that mean?"

"It means I'm here to protect you. Whatever it takes. I swear I will find a way to make it all work out."

I believed he would try. But there were still things he didn't know…and I didn't know how to tell him without putting him in an unfair and impossible situation. Not that I wouldn't deserve whatever happened. But it would hurt him—hurt us both.

"I don't deserve someone like you," I whispered, looking over his shoulder at the horizon and the sun sinking behind the trees. Somehow, the day had slipped away, and we didn't have much time left.

Vegas and all its trouble beckoned.

"That's the biggest lie I've ever heard. You deserve whatever you want. Even if that was Ronin. Although if you do want him, I'm pretty sure I'd have to kill him just to sleep at night."

I snorted. Embarrassed by such an unladylike sound, I quickly covered my mouth and nose. "Oh my God."

Rock responded by throwing back his head and laughing long and loud. I felt the throaty vibrations in my chest as my nipples bunched in response. Good or bad, I was clearly obsessed with everything about him. And so damned gone in love with him.

I leaned forward and kissed his exposed throat before sucking some of the skin between my teeth. His laugh turned to a groan as his heavily muscled arms encircled my body. I leaned into that strength—reveling in it.

"Yes, baby. Take what you want. We both need this," He murmured into my hair.

I sucked harder, uncaring of whether it would leave a mark or not. I lifted my legs and wrapped them around his waist and locked my feet behind his back. The shock of his full nudity against me brought me up short.

"You don't have any clothes on," I said, as I adjusted my position until his cock settled between my legs.

"Of course not. I'm not letting my gorgeous woman swim naked in my pool without joining her. That would be insane.

"Mmm,"' I hummed, loving the compliment, but unwilling to take my mouth off of him again. I rubbed my lips back and forth across his neck, taking in the taste of his skin combined with a little chlorine from the pool. It didn't seem like it would be sexy, but on him? Hell yes, it was sexy.

"You are such a filthy woman when you want to be, and I fucking love it." He reached between us and pinched one of my nipples until I gasped and pulled away from his neck.

"Oh my God. Rock."

"Don't you mean Sir?" He growled, pinching his fingers tighter.

"Yes, Sir!" I groaned, trying not to rub against him like a cat in heat and failing big time. I suddenly wanted him inside of me more than I wanted to breathe. Being with him did this to me every single time.

"Such a good girl," he crooned at my ear. "My good filthy girl."

Yessss.

"I need you inside me. Please." He loved it when I begged, and I loved that it made him squirm. Submitting to him and his desires always made me feel incredibly powerful.

"Then take it." We both groaned when I rubbed my pussy along the length of his cock. There were times my brazen behavior would earn me a spanking and then there were times, like this, where he wanted nothing more than for me to take what I needed.

I reached between us and positioned his cock before I eased down so the tip breached my entrance.

"Don't be a tease, Nova. If you're going to ride me, do it right." That graveled, slightly bossy chastisement tweaked my need. He always knew the exact words that would get him exactly what he wanted from me.

I slid down his shaft until he was seated fully inside me, groaning again at the stretch. With a little extra burn for good measure. I still had a hard time believing he fit, sometimes. The man had a beautiful, big cock, and I could feel every vein and ridge when he pulled back and slammed forward.

"Harder, my beautiful. Don't be shy now, we're way beyond that." He moved his hands to my ass and used that as leverage to fuck me harder.

CHAPTER 13

Rock

I was halfway to losing my goddamned mind when her inner muscles squeezed around my cock. But I didn't want to come. Not yet. I lifted her off of me and headed towards the side of the pool. We were alone, far away from all the bullshit in Vegas, and I wasn't going to rush this. It was time to finally savor what belonged to me.

"Hey!" she protested.

I ignored her complaint with nothing more than a dark look. She should have known if she was going to drive me wild, then I would wrestle that control back from her and make it even better. There were some things that would never change.

Laying her out on the deck, with her legs still dangling in the pool, I leaned forward and kissed her bare mound. I grabbed her thighs and squeezed them hard. "Spread your legs." I didn't wait for her to comply before I slid a finger past her swollen lips, teasing the silken flesh with my rough finger.

"Oh shit. Rock." She barely had my name out before she complied and gave me full access to her beautiful pussy.

"Now that's more like it." I buried my face and lapped furiously at her wet slit. One taste of her was never enough, and I planned to bring her to the brink over and over again.

The delicious scent of her arousal perfumed the twilight air. When I bought this house I'd not thought about the pool quite like this, but now that I had her here, like this, it's all I could think about. In fact, this might be my new favorite spot on the entire property.

"Fucking delicious," I grunted while continuing to lick her entire slit, while purposely avoiding the one spot that would drive her over the edge. Not yet...

FALLEN ANGEL

Instead, I added another finger alongside the first, slowly curving them to reach my favorite spot of all. The one guaranteed to make her scream. Good thing my neighbors weren't close by. She was going to put on a private show just for me.

"Yes, oh God." Her voice rose several octaves, and I smiled against her pretty pink flesh and pumped harder. Her legs shook under my hold, her hands grabbed at my shoulders, her sharp nails nipping at my skin, and whimpers fell from her lips one right after the other. "Please don't stop," she begs.

I pushed her further by sucking on her clit and pulling it into my mouth. She rocked against me, and I knew she was getting close. Just a little bit more...

When her muscles bunched one last time, I popped my mouth free and bit into her thigh, leaving her orgasm just out of reach.

"No!" she cried. "Please, Rock."

I chuckled against her skin, tickling the tender flesh while my fingers still fucked her. I could get her off without the clitoral stimulation, but it generally took longer that way, which was exactly what I wanted.

In fact...

E.M. GAYLE

I rose out of the pool and suddenly pulled her to her feet. She looked shaky and dazed as I cupped both her cheeks. "I want you so damned bad right now, beautiful."

"Then take me," she whispered, her eyes fiery and her bottom lip quivering.

"Now thats more like it."

I swept her into my arms and carried her into the house. "I know you think you know what kind of man I am, and to an extent you do. But you need to see beyond the surface. I am not my job. I just happen to be really good at it. I see things in people that others overlook. Like you for instance. You think you know what you need, but half the time I don't think you do. Otherwise you wouldn't sit in a bar every night looking for something that isn't there."

"I met *you* in a bar."

"Indeed you did, and we're both going to chalk that up to the luckiest damn night of our lives one day. It's going to give us a story to tell for years to come."

"What are you saying?"

I could practically see the fear going ballistic inside her. She wasn't ready to hear it yet. I couldn't blame her. There was a lot of shit

FALLEN ANGEL

hanging over her head that we needed to get clear of before real life could begin.

"Only that I see what you need. There's a reason you continue to risk everything for one more night with me. You need me to show you that its okay to be like this. That it's not wrong to want to surrender to someone you love. That you don't have to be alone to prove anything. But I'm here to tell you one more thing that you need to face first."

"What's that?"

"One more night will never be enough."

I shoved open the door to my bedroom and carried her over to the bed. I wanted nothing more than to fuck her blind and make her come so hard she'd never stop coming back for more, but this time I wanted it to be a little bit different. For the first time in ever we were away from everything else that weighed us both down. We were alone in a place that had no secrets to tell and nothing to hold us back.

I laid her down in the middle of my king-sized bed and came down over, pressing all of my weight onto her. I was heavy and it would be difficult to breathe, but I needed her focused on me and not whatever lived in her brain that ate at her day and night. Once I was satisfied I had

E.M. GAYLE

her completely in the moment, I reached under the headboard and produced the built in straps that would hold her down.

I proceeded to wrap them around one wrist and tugged to make sure it would not come loose or hurt her when she struggled.

"Rock, what's happening?" She didn't sound scared or concerned, only curious.

"I'm restraining you. If that's a problem let me know and I'll stop. Is it a problem?"

She stared at me for a few long seconds before she pulled her bottom lip between her teeth and shook her head.

"I know you're scared, but you don't have to be. Not of me. Not of anything."

"I'm not scared of you."

I wasn't one hundred percent sure I believed her, but that little tinge of fear was part of the thrill we both craved. Minutes later, I had her arms and legs secured, with her legs spread wide, making her completely available to me for whatever I wanted. The thrill of this moment raced down my spine and drew up my balls. Fuck. I was going to go insane if I didn't fuck her soon.

If I hadn't already been balls deep in her in the pool, I might have been able to draw this out. But I could still feel the heated grip of her muscles clenching on my dick and the sweet taste of her pussy on my tongue. It wasn't enough. Hell, it would never be enough. I wanted more.

I slid between her legs and hovered my face over her wet slit. "I love seeing you like this. All wet and ready and aching for more. I'd leave you like this all night if I could."

"That wouldn't be very nice."

"I keep telling you I'm not some kind of saint. It's not my fault you don't listen."

"Then show me."

A grin so feral I could feel it to my soul slid across my face as I thrust two fingers inside her. She was tight, but this is nothing compared to the size of my dick and she knows it. I watched and waited as the expressions on her beautiful face changed as she neared the edge of sanity, pulling on her restraints as she fought hard to get there.

"Please, Rock."

I growl in response at her weak plea. "Really, Nova? Do you even want to come?"

"Of course I do," she shrieks, gyrating on my fingers and probably praying I will touch her in just the right spot.

"Then act like it," I said as I latched my mouth

E.M. GAYLE

down on her sensitive little clit for a moment before I withdrew once again.

"Dammit. Why are you teasing me like this?"

I threw my head back and laughed, enjoying the moment more than I thought possible. She was so damned perfect. "Because I can and I will, until I hear the correct words out of your mouth."

She glared at me as if she wanted to defy me and I loved her even more for that. I pinched her clit for good measure until her mouth formed a silent O moments before she screamed.

"Don't stop, Sir. Please. Please. Please."

"Now that's more like it." Keeping the pressure of my fingers of my left hand tight, I withdrew from her body and trailed the wetness down to her ass and the tight ring of muscle just waiting for me there. "Want more?"

Her response came in the form of her flexing her hips as much as the restraint would allow so that the tip of my finger pushed its way in. I hovered there, waiting, watching her struggle to breath.

"Answer my question, sweetheart."

"Yes, please. I want more." Her voice rose several octaves halfway through the sentence, making me smile. She was beyond ready to detonate.

I pushed in about halfway and froze, letting her body accommodate to the sensation. Her legs were trembling and the pleas were falling left and right from her mouth. I had her right where I wanted her, and it felt perfect. With my dick about to explode, I was right there with her. It took all of my restraint not to drill into her asshole with fierce abandon. Instead, I took it slow and steady, teasing and taunting her with a darker pleasure she seemed to love.

"Please make me come, Rock. I don't think I can take it anymore." Hell, she probably didn't realize it but she was about to come whether I helped her get there or not. Her body was on fire and soon there would be no stopping it. What she really wanted was permission.

However, I was going to push her just a little bit more.

"Have you ever had a plug in your ass before, sweetheart?"

She shook her head, her whole body shaking now. Okay hold still. I'll be right back.

Her whimper nearly cracked my heart as I turned away from her to grab the needed supplies. I wasn't gone long, but the look on her face when I returned was priceless. She looked both devastated and needy.

"Still want more, Nova?"

"God yes," she cried, tugging again at her restraints. Watching her struggle was way more fun that it should have been. I liked seeing her crazy like this. It proved how in the moment she finally was. Nothing else mattered except us and our pleasure.

I uncapped the lube and drizzled a generous amount on her asshole, before I slowly pressed the slim silicone plug against her opening.

On a sharp intake of breath, she tensed.

"It's okay, sweetheart. Don't worry, it's a small one, barely bigger than a finger. You can definitely handle it. Do you want to keep going?"

"Will you let me come?"

Ahhh. There it was. The sweet sound of the submission I'd been waiting for.

"Of course I will. You've more than earned it."

She gave me a soft smile, and I swear that beautiful gift warmed me from the inside out. God damn I'd do anything to see that on her face every fucking day.

"Do it," she whispered, "I need you."

With only a soft push, I pressed the plug all the way and even sweeter moan fell from her lush lips, breaking the tether that held her to the ground.

"Goddamn that looks good on you." That's all I could get out before she begs me for more and it's the most incredible thing I've ever heard.

"Please, you promised."

I did indeed. In the span of a blink I was between her legs with my cock notched at her entrance and slowing working my way inside her too-tight cunt.

"I don't think it's going to work."

I smiled darkly. "Tell me to stop if you need to, but it will work. Trust me. Although we might both die from the pleasure."

To prove my point, I slid all in one one smooth push until I was buried balls deep, setting off a chain reaction we were both helpless to stop.

"I'm coming already," she screamed as the first clench of her around me robbed me of air. I wasn't going to last ten seconds at this rate because it was so far beyond incredible my brain had no words to describe it. The fact she'd gone wild fed something inside me that made me lose control as well. I stilled, took a deep breath, and held it as long as I could to regain my equilibrium. Nova was gone as I reached between our bodies and rubbed at her clit.

Watching her was like watching a runaway train. I couldn't stop admiring her as her entire body thrashed as hard as the restraints allowed. I slowly rolled my hips forward and dipped my hips so my cock would brush against her at the perfect angle. The moment it happened, her eyes rolled back in her head, and her entire body locked up. A mixture of groans, cries and screams all bounced through the room at once.

I pumped harder as her spasms continued nonstop. "I don't want this to end." I don't know if she heard me, but the words were out there.

She was mine.

The rest of the world could fuck off.

They couldn't have what wasn't theirs.

I clenched my teeth, trying to keep my orgasm under control, but it was too late. Her back arched and her hips bucked wildly, as I sank into her over and over again.

"Forever, Nova. Try to remember that. I drove into her one last time and roared as my release ripped from my body, taking everything I had and giving it to the woman underneath me. It was beyond explosive. Almost painful in its intensity, and the best damned feeling in the whole world.

By the time I could finally breath again, I looked up to see Nova barely conscious. I wanted to gloat that I'd done that to her, but I didn't have the energy left. It was all I could manage to gently pull out of her so I could remove the restraints and rub her arms and legs to ensure good circulation.

Waves of exhaustion washed over me as I cared for Nova. The stress of the job, the worry for her, all of it had built to this. We'd had to get it out in the most primal form possible. For the first time in more days that I wanted to admit, I was going to get some sleep.

CHAPTER 14

Rock

"Are you hungry?" I asked, pulling her into my side so that I could nibble at her ear. I wasn't sure I would be satiated for long. This was the first time we'd spent this much time together and I couldn't seem to get enough of her.

"Starved, actually."

I knifed forward and reluctantly let her go. "I'm sure I can create something passable for us. I had some supplies ordered when you were sleeping."

"Do you cook?"

E.M. GAYLE

"Not enough, but I can get by."

"Can I help?" She asked rolling over onto her stomach and losing the sheet in the process.

I leaned forward and slapped her tempting ass. "I'm not going to turn any help down, especially if you happen to know your way around the kitchen."

She smirked, rubbing her red cheek. "I might have cooked for myself a time or two...and taken a few lessons from Zia."

"Well, damn. Let's go then." I held my hand out for her. When she smiled up at me and placed her hand in mine, my chest got tight. She scooted off the bed and reached for the T-shirt I'd left on the chair the day before.

"Nova." There was no denying the overwhelming emotion that currently clawed at my throat making it difficult for me to say much else.

Her head popped through the neck of my shirt. "What?" Somehow, with her hair tussled, no makeup on her face, and a shirt five sizes too big for her, she managed to look both adorable and sexy as hell.

"Never mind. You ready?"

"Sure. Let's do it."

I inwardly groaned because suddenly I

164

FALLEN ANGEL

wanted to do things with her that had absolutely nothing to do with food, and I had to wait. My woman needed sustenance. We walked together from the bedroom to the kitchen in silence. It didn't seem uncomfortable or awkward like it could have been considering the consequences. I hoped that this time, we could have a conversation about the fashion show that didn't end up with us yelling at each other or screwing our brains out.

"My kitchen isn't fancy, but it should have whatever you need. When I spend time up here I tend to cook for myself instead of going out, so I've collected a decent amount of cookware and basic supplies."

"This kitchen is awesome," she said, looking in one direction after another. "Is this your pantry?" she pointed at the largest double-door cabinet across the spacious room.

"Yeah. Spices are in the drawer below the cooktop, and everything else you might need is probably in the refrigerator. Do you have any idea what you'd like to eat? I can check for the ingredients."

"I've learned a few of the basic Italian sauces, white sauce being the latest. We can make that, if that works for you." The nervous look on her

E.M. GAYLE

face almost made me laugh. She had absolutely nothing to worry about with me when it came to cooking.

"I'm happy with about anything you'd like. I'm not picky at all. Except for olives. Black, green, I hate them all." I'd seen her eat them out of her martinis on many occasions so I knew she did not have the same aversion to them that I did.

"Really? Wow. I love olives."

"I know, which is why I mentioned it. You can literally feed me anything else in the world, and even if it's not my favorite, I won't think twice about it."

"Okay. Duly noted. I will not put any olives in your food ever."

There was something in the way she said that which made me believe this would not be the last time we'd share a meal together. She'd probably meant nothing by it, but I couldn't get it out of my head. As far as I was concerned, she could stay forever.

"I was serious before about not letting you marry Ronin. If you think that makes me sound like a bully, I'll live with that."

"I'm not sure you or I have complete control in that decision."

"Why? Other than this idea that you have an

166

obligation to your family. How can your father make you do anything? He can't force you to marry."

Her body hitched a moment before she leaned into my enormous commercial-sized refrigerator that had come with the place. I'd hit a nerve. There was definitely something she wasn't telling me.

"The obligations to family aren't just perceived. It's part of who we are. It's an honor thing, and in our family, honor means more than nearly everything else."

"And was it honorable that your father had one of his men inject you with a chemical that instantly rendered you helpless so that he could kidnap you?" I slapped my hands down on the island, and she flinched. "Would it be honorable if he killed you because you couldn't deliver the diamonds?"

"Please don't yell at me, Rock. You don't understand. Family is so complicated. Especially ours."

Guilt pinged through him. He hadn't meant to yell. "Trust me, I get complicated families. However, as far as I'm concerned, your father broke whatever honor he had about family. I can't trust he won't try to snatch you again, and

E.M. GAYLE

I'm not confident being his daughter is enough to keep you alive if he does."

"I know," she said, setting the fresh carton of heavy cream down on the island next to the stove. "But that doesn't mean I can just hide from him, either. I can tell him what happened."

"You're going to tell your father that you gave the diamonds to me, but that they turned out to be fake?"

She shook her head as she gathered the rest of her supplies and turned on the burner underneath the pan she'd pulled out. "Now that would be a death warrant, for sure. But if you don't have the real diamonds, then there is only one other person who can."

It only took a moment for the answer to click. Son of a bitch. "Ronin knew about the diamonds?"

"Yes. My original plan was to give them to my father in exchange for my freedom. Only, when he turned on me, I realized nothing would change my fate with my father. I would have to marry Ronin, no matter what. I also thought at some point that maybe I could entice Ronin into a deal with those stupid gems. But that blew up in my face, too. He laughed at me. He called them trivial and practically worthless. Which is why, when I found out the truth about you, I didn't care if you had them. Hell, you could have arrested me for stealing them and I wouldn't have cared."

"But if Ronin stole them from you and switched them for fakes, then he did care about them." My mind was turning with ideas in super speed. I could barely keep up. "Do you have any idea what he would do with them?"

She slowly shook her head in tandem with the spoon she worked through her sauce. "He hates my father. I don't know why, but if I had to guess, it's something big. He's so hot and cold about our marriage that half the time I think I have nothing to do with the reason he's here."

"That's actually rather ominous. If Ronin has a hidden agenda, and it would not surprise me if he did, then we have bigger problems than I even thought." He was starting to see all the puzzle pieces laid out in his head, but how they all fit together remained a mystery. He was going to need some extra assistance to work through this.

Silence descended in the kitchen as we both got lost in our thoughts. By the time I shook myself free, Nova had finished her sauce and cooked pasta to go with it. I rounded the island

E.M. GAYLE

and placed a kiss on the top of her head. "I'm sorry. I didn't mean to ignore you."

"It didn't bother me at all. We both have a lot on our mind."

"It smells really good. Are you going to let me try it?" While the words were utterly true, it was the sight of her bare legs that had my full attention. Not to mention the fact she wore nothing underneath that shirt, which meant nothing to stop me...

"It will be ready in a few minutes."

I turned her in my arms and placed a kiss on her soft mouth this time, bending her backwards. "And what if I can't wait?" I lifted a hand to brush her hard nipples through the flimsy cotton of my shirt. My scent on her created a heady combination that was all but impossible to ignore.

"Then don't wait," she said, sounding as provocative as she did demure.

"You drive me fucking crazy. Do you know that? Lift up that shirt and bend over the counter. I'm about to fuck you so ha—"

A chime sounded in the distance at the same time my cell phone beeped.

"What was that?" she asked, looking as on the edge as I felt.

"Shit. That was a lot faster than I expected."

"What was? Rock, what's going on?"

I frowned. "It looks like what I want is going to have to wait after all. We've got company."

"Company?" she shrieked. "I thought you said no one knew where this place was."

"They didn't. At least, not until earlier this morning. I called my brother and he looped in the club. If we're going back to Vegas, we aren't doing it alone or without a plan."

"Your brother? He's here?"

"Yeah. And likely JD and the whole club. You should probably put some clothes on. Preferably something that covers everything. I don't need any of those horny fuckers eyeballing my woman and pissing me off."

"Do you mean the motorcycle club that you used to belong to? They are all here, right now." She looked shellshocked, although I didn't know what the big deal was. They were just men. Most of them were good guys, and I could count on all of them to help.

"You don't have anything to worry about. I don't think anyone bites. At least they better fucking not."

"Oh my God." She backed away from me. "Why didn't you warn me?"

"Seriously, relax Nova. They're here to help,

and at this point we really need it. There's no need to freak out. No one else knows where we are."

"But it's your dad. I can't meet the family like this."

I clamped my lips to hold back my laugh. I hadn't thought of it like that, and I shouldn't be amused at her distress. But it was pretty fucking funny watching her freak out about meeting my father. He had enough goddamn sense not to say anything to her she wouldn't like.

He'd better.

CHAPTER 15

Nova

I disappeared into the bedroom to search for something appropriate to wear, cursing Rock under my breath the whole time. I kind of wanted to throttle him. I didn't think I was ready to meet his father at the moment, and especially not under these circumstances.

"Damn, son. What smells so good in here?" The question sounded gruff and gravelly all at the same time. It caused the hairs to stand up on the back of my neck. I couldn't make out Rock's

E.M. GAYLE

response as I closed the door behind me, but nothing was going to erase the nerves now.

I guess all things considered, it shouldn't really matter what his family thought about me. It's not like Rock and I were girlfriend and boyfriend. I had a fiancé, although why I had to keep reminding myself of that, I couldn't fathom. Plus, Rock had made his feelings on the matter of Ronin pretty damned clear. I wasn't sure what the hell I believed in right now, but I did think he meant what he'd said.

I looked through his closet and his drawers in search of something I could potentially wear, and came up with nothing that wouldn't look ridiculous. I retreated to the bathroom where I'd left my clothes after my shower last night. They were a wrinkled hot mess, but they were going to have to do. A few minutes later I was dressed and ready to go, until I caught myself in the mirror and froze.

Without makeup I looked like a teenager. I'd learned early on after leaving home that in order to be taken seriously I couldn't look like a fifteen-year-old. If only Rock had thought to pack my toiletry bag before kidnapping me.

I snickered. My train of thought had veered into the ridiculous and I needed to rein it in. It

FALLEN ANGEL

didn't matter what those men out there thought of me. I wasn't here to win them over. I didn't even want to ask for their help. To do so made me uncomfortable at best. As much as I tried to ignore it, Cullotta blood still ran through my veins, and our privacy had been drilled into me from early childhood.

I could share Nova with the world without so much as a blink of an eye, but Catherine... Well, that was a different story. With a final smirk at myself in the window I tipped my body forward and gathered my long hair on top of my head. Thank goodness I always kept a ponytail holder in my pocket at all times. I fished my hair through the band several times and twisted it into a messy bun. It didn't help as much as I had hoped, but at least it was something.

With my head held high, and a heavy dose of false bravado, I waltzed into the middle of complete chaos.

Men sprawled across every sitting surface of the room and on into the dining room. The television had been turned on to—football. Of course it was. And every last one of them had a bowl of pasta drowning in my white sauce.

"I hope you left some for me."

All heads turned, and I nearly swallowed my

own tongue at the intensity of all of their focus on me. They were all dressed almost identically. Jeans, T-shirt, black vest with patches on it and some variety of boots. Something clicked in my mind, and I filed a mental picture of this moment away for the next time I had a sketch pad in my hands. Other than the clothes they wore, every single one of them looked nothing like the others. There were beards of varying sizes, from not much more than a five o'clock shadow to well beyond their chins.

If there was one thing about all of them that I could say, it was this was not a ragtag bunch of biker losers like I might have imagined if I was thinking stereotypes. These were big, strapping men no one would want to meet in a back alley alone, but they were also smoking hot in the most rugged, testosterone-filled way.

"I made sure they left you a plate," Rock walked up to my side and wrapped his arm around my waist, pulling me close. "You still hungry?"

I nodded, feeling a little overwhelmed and unusually shy. "Let's grab you some food, and then I'll introduce you to everyone. If you wait too long, I'm worried they are going to eat everything that isn't nailed down."

A couple of men voiced their dissent, but it was all done with snickers and eye rolls. Before I could get my bearings, an older man with a touch of gray hair at his temples and a few strands of silver in his beard approached. "I'm JD. President of the club. I wish we were meeting under better circumstances."

He held out his hand and despite my nerves I gripped his hand in a firm handshake. "Nova," I said, smiling as best I could in the face of this intimidating yet good-looking man. It was easy to see where Rock got his looks. And it was easy to tell they were father and son. They were almost carbon copies of the same person, one with a few more wrinkles than the other. "I'm sorry you had to come all this way. If I had known you were coming, I would have made more of an effort with the food.

"Are you kidding? That sauce is incredible." He rubbed his stomach. "Ate more than I needed to, but I couldn't resist."

"I'll be sure to pass on the compliment to my friend Zia. The recipe is hers. She's a freaking goddess in the kitchen."

JD eyed me with an intensity that made me want to squirm. I didn't know what he was

E.M. GAYLE

trying to figure out, but I was probably better off not knowing.

"C'mon," Rock urged me away from his father. "You need to eat before we get down to business. The game is in the last quarter, and while nothing gets them away from a Seahawks game, the minute it's over, they are going to be ready for action."

As if on cue, something on the television must have happened because many of them jumped out of their seats, yelling at the tv. They were definitely enthusiastic about their football.

"Don't mind them. Twelves are a bit obsessed."

"Twelves?" I hated to admit I had no idea what he was talking about, but football wasn't a game I had a lot of experience with.

"That's what the Seattle Seahawk fans are called. The Twelfth man. Their enthusiasm is well-known."

"You sound more and more like you miss being there," I pointed out as I dished up a small bowl of pasta with sauce. The aroma slammed into me and my stomach growled. It was taking all my control not to dive face first into this food.

He shrugged. "Sometimes I do. But I can be a

twelve, here. Seahawks need more fans from other states."

"Hmmm," I hummed as I scooped a spoonful of noodles drenched in the creamy cheese sauce. I groaned with delight.

"Fuck, Nova. You eat your pasta like you fuck. I'm going to have to sit here and hide my hard-on now."

I glanced around to see if anyone had heard him, but all the men had their full attention on the big screen tv. I didn't know what to say. I could already feel the heat in my face likely staining my cheeks bright red.

"So is this what normal life is like for you? Food, family and football. And a one-track mind about sex?"

"Actually no. At least not anymore. It's been years since I've sat down and watched a game with anyone but myself." He tilted the beer he'd picked up in Houston's direction. "Although I have had a meal with Houston and Izzy if that counts."

"A meal? As in just one? And yes, I do think it counts."

"Yeah, just one—so far. We were kind of estranged for a while, but we're working on it.

What about you? Besides your father, is there anyone in your family you spend time with?"

I wanted to squirm under his too knowing gaze. I knew he wasn't trying to interrogate me, but I couldn't help feeling like I was under some sort of microscope every time he asked me about my life.

"No. My father forbade me from having any contact with my siblings. Although I have spoken to my sister several times by phone. She takes orders from my father about as well as I do."

A pang of regret pinged in my chest. Practically since the moment I'd woken here in Rock's house, I'd barely thought of her and what she must be going through. I had to try and reach her again to see if anything for her had changed. In all the chaos I kept forgetting the one person who really needed my attention.

"Carina. She's about five years younger than you are, right?"

I nodded, realizing I didn't need to say anything else. We both knew what that meant in my father's world. "I'm worried about her. My father tried threatening her as leverage against me. While I don't think he'd hurt her since she would be considered a valuable asset, I'm worried I haven't heard from her."

FALLEN ANGEL

"She's fine," he lowered his voice. "I mean, physically that is. I can't speak to her mental health since we haven't spoken to her."

My head snapped back. "What? What do you mean she is fine? How do you know?"

He stared back at me without saying a word, and after a few minutes, I realized what he meant. "Is my whole family under FBI surveillance?"

He didn't answer that question either. Which meant only one thing.

"Dammit, Rock. Why didn't you tell me? Do you have any idea how worried I've been?" My words, while whispered, were harsh and angry. "I thought you wanted to be honest?" I clamped my mouth shut the minute I said those words. I had no right. Not when I'd left out my own secrets I was afraid to tell. But dammit, this was my sister.

"I'm already way past the line of what I should and shouldn't share. Cut me some slack."

He was right. I should have just asked if he knew anything about her. He couldn't read minds, and it wasn't fair for me to assume. "I'm sorry. Obviously I'm on edge more than usual."

He lifted his hand and stroked a finger down my cheek. "You don't need to apologize.

E.M. GAYLE

We're both feeling the stress of this. When this is all over, I can't wait for you and me to get away." I closed my eyes against his touch. I wanted to believe so badly that a future for us was possible, but I couldn't afford to get my hopes up.

"Get a room," someone yelled from across the room.

"Shut up, Axel." Rock grumbled. "Asshole."

Everyone laughed, which eased some of the tension, but as the television was turned off and the men moved to the dining room where we sat, I realized it was time to get serious.

Rock broke the ice with a question addressed to JD. "How's the background on Ronin going?"

I nearly choked on my drink.

"Tel is working on it." The man at the far end of the table with his head buried in his computer grunted. Tel, I assumed. "We don't have anything useful yet, but if there's something there, we'll find it. However, we did bring the equipment you asked about."

My eyebrows raised as Tel produced a small bag that he dumped on the table without even looking up from his screen. I had no idea what the scattered items were, but they definitely looked like expensive, hi-tech equipment.

FALLEN ANGEL

"What is it?" I finally asked, wanting to understand what was happening.

"Listening devices, recorders, voice and motion activators, GPS trackers, electronic signal jammers, etc. etc. etc. Anything you could possibly need to have eyes and ears in places we can't legally be, and whatever it takes to give us an advantage over them. I've even got some software for your phone and tablet that works like an app and can keep us in the know."

"For…?" This wasn't at all what I had imagined was going to happen. Although we did live in a pretty high-tech world, so I should not have been surprised.

"If you're going back to Vegas, then we are going to make sure we have you covered every single second. I refuse to take chances we don't have to. I'd prefer if you stayed here until this was all over, but I heard you loud and clear about the show. But this part is non-negotiable."

I shrugged. "Okay."

He continued as if he hadn't heard me. "It's either this or you aren't going anywhere. Seriously, Nova, I want no argument about this."

All the men looked at each other for a moment before they busted out laughing.

Rock glowered at them.

E.M. GAYLE

I placed my hand over his to get his attention. "I'm not stupid. I won't refuse your help or your direction."

"Okay then, let's introduce you to all the guys so you know the team. We're all going to be in this together."

Rock proceeded to give me the names, or nicknames, of the men in the club, and while I knew I wouldn't remember them all, I was pretty sure I would remember their faces. Some looked at me with kindness, some wariness and others indifference, but they all reiterated their club's commitment to taking down Anthony Cullotta, while keeping me safe at the same time.

"Is there a plan?" I asked.

"The plan is to go after Ronin. Since we don't expect your father to make his move until after the show, we're going to use that as our chance to go after Ronin and the diamonds."

"I seriously doubt he's just going to hand them over because you ask."

JD chuckled. "Who said anything about asking?"

"You're going to steal them back?" No one said anything, but the looks they gave each other were all the answer I needed. "Do we even know where they are?"

FALLEN ANGEL

JD's second in command, Axel, stepped forward. "Ronin made one big mistake, and it gave us the opportunity and the extra incentive to make sure we knew every single move he made. He confronted JD when you were missing and tried to pump him for information. That got our attention, and let's just say for the sake of our Federal Agent here, that we've paid attention to everything he's done since then."

Rock sighed. "I think we're well beyond the letter of the law in this case. Besides, you don't have to 'say it' for me to know you're referring to a whole host of potential crimes. A little B&E perhaps?"

Axel shrugged and no one else elaborated, leaving me and Rock to draw our own conclusions.

"So you do know where they are?" I didn't want to assume, but I did feel hopeful.

"It's likely to be one of two places. His safe at The Sinclair or on his person. We have to cover both possibilities since we don't know his exact plans for the day of the show."

"He is still acting like we're getting married, even though we know that's not happening…"

"Definitely not happening." Rock rasped, his

hand going around my waist to pull me tight against his side.

"So you're planning to break—"

"Okay, that part I *do not* want the details of." Rock interrupted, his face hardening. "Suffice it to say, we expect he will make a move, most likely during the after party when everyone is still too busy to notice and when security will be focused on a much smaller area of the hotel."

"Most of my men will be scattered throughout the event areas, including backstage to provide extra security as well as provide extra eyes and ears for movement of the target. Tel will be providing point from his computer since we'll be utilizing all the tech as well."

"I'll make sure they have the necessary passes to give them the freedom they need. I just hope you're right. Ronin isn't stupid."

"You're right, he's not. But he also knows that both me and the club are after Anthony, not him. Legally, I can't touch Ronin."

"Which is why we do what we do."

I wanted to ask JD exactly what that meant, but I had a feeling I was better off not knowing. Plus, my mind was trying to process all of this information and the possible scenarios so I could focus on the big picture.

FALLEN ANGEL

When that was done, and I had a moment kind of alone with Rock, I couldn't keep my curiosity contained any longer. "Is there some reason these men all seem to hate my father, or is this just some sort of club thing they do? Because honestly, I don't understand why these men want to help me. They don't know me."

"I'm sure you noticed JD looks a little rough. Black eye, stitches in a few places, cuts and bruises."

I nodded. A pit formed in my stomach as I jumped to conclusions. I had noticed, but I didn't want to be too forward and ask.

"Your father couldn't get to me without getting his ass arrested, so he went for my family. Which was about the dumbest thing he could have done. Attacking an MC president is one of the most asinine things someone in his position could do. I don't know if his ego is out of control or what, but he basically signed on for a war."

My eyes widened at his words, but I managed to keep my mouth from dropping open. That did sound incredibly stupid on my father's part *and* out of character. "Oh my God. I am so sorry. I had no idea."

"Why would you? You aren't responsible for

your father's actions. The man has made his bed, and he will soon have to lie in it."

I shifted uncomfortably in the chair I sat in. "What will they do to him?" I probably didn't want to know the answer to that question, but I couldn't seem to resist asking it. "Please don't sugarcoat your answer or avoid it. I need to know the truth. I want to be prepared for what's coming."

"I am not sure you can be totally prepared for what might happen, but I get that you want to. I would feel the same way." He cleared his throat and nodded his head to the patio doors that led out to the pool. "How about we go outside and finish this conversation."

I nodded, following his gaze towards the men sitting too close for comfort. Rock led me outside, and I breathed a heavy sigh of relief when the slider door closed behind us and we were alone outside. I breathed in a gulp of fresh air and held it for a moment before releasing it slow. I didn't realize how much I needed to this until right that moment.

"Tell me," I urged. "Please."

"If JD has his way, your father won't live another week. Under different circumstances, he might consider eye for an eye style of retaliation, but we all know that it will never end there. If they attack your father, and they will, it will be one battle after another until the innocent casualties become unbearable. So JD is going to do whatever it takes to end it with one confrontation."

"And you're okay with that?" What kind of FBI agent did that make him? I rubbed at my arms to hide the sudden chill bumps popping up on my skin. And who the hell was I to judge?

"Hell, no. I'm not okay with that. I want nothing more than to see your father in court, where he has to answer for his crimes the hard way. His death at JD's hands, while effective getting him off the streets and making the world a safer place, is not the answer. It's the easy way out."

I didn't know about that. Killing someone it wasn't….

"So you want him locked up?"

"I want him to be punished for all the shit he's done and the people he's hurt and will hurt. I'm not a judge or a jury. How he pays isn't my job. Although I won't lie, when I saw that needle go into your neck, I reacted in pure rage. If your father had been there, I might have killed him. Hell, I still might. But I'm not letting the club

E.M. GAYLE

take over this fight for me. That I can guarantee. I will see this through all the way to the end. Whatever that happens to be." He squeezed my hands. "We'll do it together."

I wasn't sure what to think. Or what I could say. If his stance on this was as rigid as it sounded then how did I ever stand a chance if/when he learned the truth about me? My stomach roiled just thinking about it. I never wanted to see that look of disgust on his face turned towards me. I wouldn't survive it. And this was exactly why we were not going to end up together.

Our lives were too different. In our family, the apple wasn't permitted to fall too far from the tree. Our life was ingrained in us. He mistakenly thought locking my father up would change something, when I knew it would not. There was only one thing that would give my life a different outcome, and I wasn't sure I had the guts to do it.

I could, however, honor all the commitments I had made, and maybe help Rock get what he wanted. At least professionally. I owed him that much. He deserved the truth too, but I couldn't— I just couldn't.

"I think it's time," I whispered.

He leaned closer, and I breathed his scent deep to memorize it. I was going to need this to get me through the coming days.

"We could stay a little longer."

I shook my head. No. If I stayed much longer, it would be too hard to leave. Too many people were counting on me to show up. Now in more ways than one. I was going to see this through, no matter what sacrifices had to be made.

"It's time to take me home."

CHAPTER 16

Nova

I looked out over the rapidly filling auditorium and imagined how, in less than an hour, the space would be packed with people who wanted to see my designs.

The press would take endless pictures and splash them across social media, celebrities would take note and hopefully place orders, and then there would be the critics, who with a few keystrokes on their phone could make or break an event like this.

I already had more than enough accolades and clients in my store, but this show was next

E.M. GAYLE

level for me. My time in New York had taught me a lot, but I'd never quite gotten where I wanted to be. Not until I moved back to Vegas, and took the time to build a social media presence for me and my designs.

One viral video later, and I had celebrities contacting me for more requests than I could handle, and the interest of a businessman looking to round out his exclusive hotel with something new and fresh. It was thrilling and exciting, but this…

My own show.

A few hours ago I was worried I'd miss it all, but Rock had lived up to his promise, and here I was, poised to showcase my life's dream, and blow up my entire world at the same time.

"Nova, you're needed backstage. There's a problem with the lineup."

I inwardly groaned. Of course there was a problem. It was to be expected.

I turned toward Trina, who would coordinate everything along with the support of the rest of the team. There was no doubt in my mind we would make it all work. I'd hand chosen her based on her strengths and my weaknesses. We complemented each other perfectly. However, no matter how well we planned, things were still going to happen.

"What is it?"

"One of the dresses you have scheduled to show is missing, and another doesn't fit the model assigned to wear it."

I took a deep breath and followed her backstage. "Okay, show me which dress is missing. I made duplicates of everything, just in case. I can retrieve whatever we need from the vault."

"Perfect." Trina tapped a few things on her tablet and then turned it to show me. She and I were the only ones allowed any electronic devices backstage. All other cellphones and tablets had been confiscated until after the event. Tonight was the big reveal of these designs, and we couldn't risk anything getting out early. I made a mental note of the dress.

"Now, which model and which dress is not working out?" Trina led me over to one of the dressing rooms, knocked before she entered, opened the door, and ushered me inside.

Immediate chaos greeted me. There were people everywhere. Models in varying stages of undress, hairdressers and make-up artists working their magic, technicians testing out different

E.M. GAYLE

lighting and talking each of the women through the process. It might have looked like a free for all, but it was all actually very organized and orchestrated.

The energy of it all was exciting, and the excitement in the air was contagious.

As soon as I saw the model wearing one of my daywear dresses, I needed no further explanation. I walked over to the big whiteboard with a square for every outfit. The sketches of each, were miniature drawings of my original works. I scanned through the lineup and the models assigned to each one until a solution presented itself. "Let's switch out model number 3 for this one. The cut of that dress will fit Gigi better, and Michelle works for anything in the collection. Make sure they both understand the change in lineup, and get an extra run-through during the final rehearsal."

Trina made notes and Gigi looked relieved instead of on the verge of tears.

"What's next?" I asked as we headed back into the heart of the backstage area that had also filled with people.

"That's it for now. Although I'm sure something else will come up soon." Trina started to turn away when she suddenly turned back. "Oh. Your dress was delivered by security and put in the closet of your office. Do you want to try it on and make sure it's okay? It's the only one that hasn't been fitted today."

"Sure. I'll do that now." Of course we'd had multiple try on sessions, but that didn't mean anything as evidenced by Gigi's issue. Every time a seamstress got their hands on a dress, things changed.

I headed into my office and came to an immediate halt. "What are you doing here?"

Sitting behind my desk with his feet up and his phone at his ear, he looked entirely too comfortable in my space for my own good. I also didn't care if I was interrupting something important. I had not offered him my office for a reason, and if he was going to insist on staying by my side the entire time, he could do it elsewhere.

He clicked off his phone and I imagined how the party on the other end of the line felt being hung up on without so much as a goodbye. "Wouldn't the question of the day be where the hell have you been?" He didn't make to move from my chair or even remove his shoes from my desk. "Although that is actually a stupid question, isn't it? I think we both know exactly where you were and who you were fucking."

E.M. GAYLE

I so did not have time for this confrontation. Even if it was completely necessary. "You shouldn't be back here. Especially not with that." I pointed at his cellphone. "All electronics have been banned backstage until the show ends. No pictures or recordings of any kind are allowed."

He smirked. "That's what you think is important in all this?" He waved his phone in my general direction. "I have no reason to take pictures, Nova. I'm not into fashion espionage."

I rolled my eyes at his sarcasm. I wasn't in the mood for anymore of his digs. I got it. He didn't give a crap.

"And we're not married, yet, so I don't have to do as I'm told."

His laid-back expression disappeared and his eyes narrowed to angry slits. "I'm getting tired of this. Have you seen your father, yet?" he asked.

The hairs on the back of my neck rose as I bit back my retort to the first part of his statement. "No. Should I have?"

"Maybe. I've heard he's looking for you."

I bet he was. "What on earth for? He's got to know I'm not going to talk to him after the last time."

"That's exactly what I told him. But he seems hellbent. Do you know why?"

I took a deep breath. This was it. "I think he knows about the diamonds."

Ronin narrowed his eyes. "Is that what your *lover* told you?"

Withholding a sigh wasn't easy. I understood that I was playing with fire every time I went anywhere near Rock, but until Ronin and I married, I resisted his control over my life.

"The information about my father did come from Rock. But that's not all he told me," I hesitated, waiting for a sign from him that he was interested in what I had to say. I carefully stood as still as possible, doing the best I could not to fidget or show any other outward sign of nervousness. When he said nothing, and didn't even look up from looking at his phone, I continued. "He claims the diamonds I gave him aren't real. He's pissed and ready to arrest me for fraud if I don't produce the real ones."

He still didn't look at me, but I did see the tic of his jaw muscle for a split second. Despite that, he wasn't going to make it easy. He was the logical choice for the thief, but I had nothing to prove that, and I doubted very much he would confess.

"Sounds like you got played. If the diamonds

E.M. GAYLE

aren't real you went to a lot of trouble to get them for nothing."

"You might think. Except I had the diamonds I took verified. They were as real as they come."

He finally looked up at me, his face one hundred percent passive. "You let someone steal them. From your hotel safe? Jesus, Nova. That's why someone like you shouldn't be playing the game. You are incompetent."

I threw up my hands. "What fucking game? What are you talking about?"

"Language, Nova. Some find it sexy when their women talk like trash, I do not." I caught him narrowing his eyes at me again in that frustrated look of his and it made me want to strangle him. How dare he judge me for the way I spoke? The asshole did things one hundred times worse.

"I know you took them." I hadn't been sure until right that moment if I would make that accusation, but he clearly thought I was an idiot if didn't think I could put two and two together. "What I don't know, is why. When I wanted to broker a deal with you in exchange for them, you said they were worthless to you. So why take them?"

He stood and crossed the room, looking

FALLEN ANGEL

down at me as if I were a child that needed to be indulged. He even went so far as to pat my head. "Because I could. I took your assurances that they were valuable to your father, and anything valuable to him is valuable to me."

"But why? I would have given them to you. I only wanted my freedom. That seems like an easy price to pay."

A harsh laugh erupted over my head, the sound of it grating down my nerves. I wanted him to tell me more, but I could feel the pit in my stomach growing by the second. Whatever he deigned to tell me wasn't going to be pleasant.

"Honestly, your freedom means nothing to me. But you are a key player and that makes you fair game."

"You are not making any sense. Why are you really here? Would it kill you to be honest?" I blew out a breath and threw up my hands. "Oh, who am I kidding? Of course it would. It's all part of the game."

"That's rich, coming from you, darling. You can't seem to tell the truth no matter the consequences. Now you'll just have to live with them."

My blood chilled at his words. I'd been as honest as I knew how. And yet somehow, it wasn't enough. But how?

E.M. GAYLE

It dawned on me then. My secrets were not my secrets anymore. "You already knew."

"That the man you married five years ago is dead? Of course I did. Only he didn't die from a heart attack. That much is obvious. You and your father weren't fooling anyone. Tell me, though. Did my grandfather die before or after he took your precious, overpriced virginity?"

I reeled. No one was supposed to know anything. Not even the marriage, let alone his... death. My father had promised. There had only been three people there that night. One of them had talked.

Wait.

"What did you say?" *Grandfather?*

"You heard me quite clearly. Don't pretend you didn't."

"Who told you?" I may have been shaking uncontrollably, but that didn't mean my mind didn't work. In fact, it went in to hyperdrive as I imagined the worst.

He smiled slowly, his eyes turning downright devilish in their intensity as he stared down at me. "You did."

My legs buckled as I struggled to stay upright. This was too much. *He* was too much. "Get out," I screamed. I was beyond caring about my

202

FALLEN ANGEL

precious facade. I would call security and have him thrown out if that's what it took.

He chuckled, another hateful sound that slithered up my spine and neck. He took one step closer and wrapped his hand around the back of my neck. I struggled to free myself with no luck. "I'll go for now, darling. But I won't be far." He released my neck with a slight shove, and I grabbed my desk to remain standing. "If nothing else, I need to protect my investment. Remember that. You've been bought and sold. Anything that happens tonight changes nothing. I'll be close by, and after the show, I intend to collect."

CHAPTER 17

Nova

By the time the ten-minute warning knock sounded on my door, I'd managed to dress and fix my face. The dress, with its neckline that plunged nearly to my waist, where it was fastened to the skirt with a diamond encrusted medallion had turned out better than I'd hoped. The silhouette was designed to flatter any figure, and I still believed it would be the crown jewel in my collection.

Internally, however, I was a mess, with more potholes than a backroads highway. Because I didn't know how to process Ronin's revelations,

E.M. GAYLE

I'd shoved them as deep as they would go and forged ahead.

The show must go on. That was the saying, after all. Although I'd happily punch the originator in the mouth right about now.

My phone had blown up after my fiancé's departure with messages from Rock, but since I wasn't ready to deal with that mess, I'd had to ignore those too. So I'd locked up my device with the rest of the crew's. Thanks to his little app on my tablet, he'd heard every word Ronin had said, and I couldn't face him or his righteous indignation. In a bare five-minute exchange, my soul had been stripped down to the bones and every secret I feared had been laid bare.

All but one...

I smoothed my hands along my hips, even though the dress was already perfect. My nerves were shot, and I needed something to pull myself together. Time maybe, but that was the one commodity I didn't have. I reached for the earpiece that would allow me to communicate with Trina for the rest of the night and shoved it in place.

I had to get out of this room and out of my head before I had a nervous breakdown. I stepped into my shoes and headed out and into the now massive chaos. The number of people backstage seemed to have exploded, running in every direction. There were cameramen at the edge of the curtain and girls lining up in what looked like a frantic panic.

I rushed in their direction, ready to put out whatever fire that had them all ready to run. "What's going on?"

"Michelle's dress is caught in the zipper and I don't think we can get it out without ripping the fabric and we have about ninety seconds until she has to walk." The normally calm Trina did not look calm. Her fingers were shaking as she fought to free the dress.

"It's okay. I've got this. You make sure everyone else is lined up and ready, Lois and I will handle Michelle's dress." I glanced at the head seamstress who also looked ready to pass out any second from the stress. Trina nodded and went to work while I stepped forward to take over. The fabric had gotten jammed pretty damned good and the zipper teeth had already snagged their way into the fabric. I was going to have to tear the dress to fix it.

"I need some small scissors and safety pins," I ordered. Lois grimaced and reached into the many pockets of her vest and fanny pack. I had

E.M. GAYLE

no doubt whatever I needed would be in there. Our seamstress was always prepared for anything. In a few seconds she produced both a pair of sharp, small snips and a handful of safety pins in an assortment of sizes. I snatched the scissors from her and began the careful task of cutting around the zipper without stabbing Michelle's skin. "Lois, open the safety pins and get them ready." We didn't have much time and I needed to conserve every second.

"Sure thing," she answered.

"Michelle, hold still. I don't want to stab you."

The model laughed tightly. "Don't worry about me, I'll be fine."

"That may be, but I'd like to avoid getting any blood on the dress. That's not exactly the look we are going for."

I snipped the last of the stuck fabric and held out the scissors to exchange for the pins.

"Thirty seconds," our stage director yelled. The girls around us sucked in sharp breaths.

"Don't worry, we've got this. We're not going to miss the timing on the opening sequence." I used the safety pins to marry the two pieces of sliced fabric back together and double pinned it through the zipper lining.

"Ten seconds." This time the warning came at

a lower volume and I could see the director counting down with his fingers. The lights dimmed, and the first song I'd selected for the show began to play.

"Just breathe, and listen to the music. Follow your cues and everything will be perfect." Trina reassured the women as I fished the final pin through the fabric.

"3…2…"

I snapped the last one closed and smoothed the fabric as best I could. "Okay, you're good to go, Michelle."

"1…"

"Thank you," she whispered as she headed through the curtain and started her first turn down the runway. From this angle, the spotlights blinded me, making it difficult for me to make out much more than the girls beginning their walks, perfectly timed.

"The second sequence girls are lined up and ready to go. We need to look them over for any adjustments." Trina stood next to me, urging everyone into place.

I stepped away from the curtain and double checked the backstage monitor instead. I motioned for the girls to move forward as I watched Michelle stop, face right, then left, and

E.M. GAYLE

spin to head back our way. I breathed a marginal sigh of relief One sequence underway, only seven more to go.

After some minor adjustments with a steamer and a curling iron, the second sequence was also on the way. I watched on the monitor again, eager to see the crowd response. Trina stood by my side making furious notes on her tablet as each girl passed the main camera.

"They look really good," she sighed. "You've outdone yourself this time."

As much as I wanted to revel in her compliment, it would have to wait until later. We still had a lot to do.

"I know. I know. Back to work." Trina ran off to do just that, and I followed her with a big smile on my face despite everything.

Halfway through the third sequence, I was beginning to believe everything would be all right. Despite a few minor issues, the models were handling everything like the pros they were. They made my job easy and my clothes look good. Judging by the faces in the crowd, I'd say they were enjoying them—

My muscles tensed as one of the cameramen scanned the crowd. Was that? I moved closer to the monitor to see if I could get a better look.

FALLEN ANGEL

Sure enough. My father sat in the crowd, a scowl etched across his face.

Fuck. Fuck. Fuck.

As long as Anthony Cullotta lived, my nightmare would never end. I understood JD's point. He would never give up. Never stop going after what he wanted. He was like a rabid dog, determined to bite you with no care that it would be lethal. If Rock put him in jail it would never end. He'd either find a way out, or he'd run the business from his cell. My brothers would be his puppets. My sister would be sold for more power. It would never end.

Then I saw the person sitting next to him, and nearly lost my lunch. What the hell were my mother and sister doing here? What the hell was this? Was he so desperate he would try to pull something here?

Of course he was. How could I ever believe otherwise? He'd already tried to snatch me backstage. I searched the crowd for any of the MC club or Rock. I knew they were close by. No matter what Rock thought of me now, he wouldn't abandon his case. He was going to protect his father from jail by sending my family instead.

I strained to see them better. My mother

looked miserable. Her hands were clenched in her lap, and her mouth was pinched like she'd just sucked a lemon or something. She didn't want to be here. Carina looked nervous. She was chewing on her bottom lip and tapping her foot against her chair. I needed to get word to someone about this turn of events. If they tried to make a move on my father, she could get caught in the crossfire.

And somewhere out there was Ronin, too. Was he seeing what I was seeing? Probably. That bastard saw everything. I'd been so naive thinking I could ever deal with him. Anger coursed through me as my options for what to do next dwindled. I had to keep going and pretend that evil wasn't lurking in every corner of the auditorium. Why the hell did I leave my tablet behind?

Fear flooded my bloodstream. I needed to stick to the plan and trust in Rock. My job was to keep everything going as normal and make sure all the high-tech gear remained in place backstage. I had to go back for my tablet. It was time to stop being an idiot.

I raced back to my office, keeping an eye out for anyone I didn't recognize along the way. I punched in the code and shoved through my door and slammed it closed behind me. The fear instilled from seeing my father flooded me with adrenaline as I crossed quickly to the safe box where I'd placed all the electronics. I opened it as quickly as my shaky hands would allow and fished around for my tablet. I pulled several out that were not mine and shoved them back inside. I reached for another, and pulled it out, relieved to see this one was mine. I jerked it free from the box, and something else flew from the box and landed on the floor.

I bent down to retrieve it, and discovered a small black velvet bag.

What the shit?

It could not be.

I untied the string holding it closed and with shaking hands, upended the contents across my tablet. A group of gems sparkled in the light as I stood with my mouth dropped open, total shock coursing through me. How in the hell had these ended up here? I didn't need to count them to know.

Thirty-six illegal gems worth millions of dollars were now sitting in my office backstage at a fashion show secured in a box that only I should have the combination to.

E.M. GAYLE

Was someone trying to set me up? Not fucking someone. Just one person.

Ronin. The bastard. But why?

And what the hell was I going to do about it? I could not keep them here. Rock and I had banged our heads against the wall this afternoon trying to come up with a way to get these back from Ronin, and he'd dumped them in my office. My head was swimming with questions and no answers. All I could think about was how he kept saying we were playing a game. What game?

Think, Nova.

There had to be an explanation. I scooped the diamonds back into the bag and shut the lockbox. I absolutely could not keep them here. If the wrong person found them, I'd be screwed or worse. Is that what Ronin was trying to do?

Did he plan to sic my father on me, which in turn, would turn the feds on him and then there was the whole MC waiting in the wings to do their part.

I started to shove them in my pocket and realized that would be even worse than the safe. I could not be caught red-handed with these things. I turned left and right, looking for somewhere to hide them. Nowhere would be good enough if someone came here to search. I could try and get upstairs and get them back in my safe, but that didn't feel right either. Ronin had already taken them from there once. When they weren't found here, that was the second place they'd look.

I glanced into the mirror and backed away from the look on my face. Abject terror did not look good on me. I wasn't the greatest at hiding anything. Under pressure? Forget it. Other than my pocket, there was nowhere else to put them for now. I wasn't even wearing a bra to stuff them in. This dress was held in place with padding and tape.

Except...

The jeweled medallion that held the top to the bottom was covered in faux diamonds. Could I somehow possibly... I looked down and prodded at the gems. One easily popped off, leaving the prong still attached to the dress behind. Oh my God. Could I? I searched my room for supplies. A needle and thread? I shook my head. No. No. No. Way too complicated and it wouldn't work. I probably had some pliers that might bend the prongs around each one. A glance at the clock told me I definitely did not have time for this. That's when I saw it at the bottom of the middle drawer. My glue gun.

E.M. GAYLE

Hell yes. That would totally work. I dug further through fabric swatches, buttons, and pins until I found a box of glue sticks. There was prepared, and then there was insane. Thank God I saved everything. I plugged in the gun, reached for my makeup bag, and fished through there until I came out with my tweezers. I then sat down in the chair and began plucking the diamonds one by one from the medallion, counting them as I went until I hit thirty-six. Grabbing the pouch, I dumped the real diamonds onto my dressing table and grabbed the first one.

How long had I been gone? Trina would be looking for me. My hands shook as I placed a dab of hot glue on the back of the first gem and pressed it into place, holding it there for a few seconds to ensure it set. To my relief, when I released it, it stayed in place. Not that I doubted the ability of my glue gun. We'd hemmed gowns with guns at the last minute, and every one of them had held up. Still.

As if on cue, a knock sounded on my door. "Nova. Are you in there?"

"Yeah. Just a minute." I shoved the fake crystals into the pouch and tucked them under my

FALLEN ANGEL

makeup bag before I rushed to the door and answered it, only opening it a crack.

"What's up?" I could see the stage director and Trina both standing there, looking worried as hell.

"There's some men here with badges asking for you. They say they have a warrant."

"A warrant for what? What kind of craziness is happening? Can't they see we are in the middle of a fashion show? They will have to come back." By this time, I was shaking so hard, I thought my bones were going to rattle. The whole thing was out of this world crazy. I tried to take a breath and came up short.

"You need to come out here and talk to them. They are insistent."

"Tell them to contact Rock Reed with the FBI. I'm sure he can handle this."

"Nova," Trina whispered through the door. "They *are* the FBI, and they are big and scary and not friendly at all. Something is really wrong."

I tried to swallow around the lump now firmly lodged in my throat. I couldn't breathe, could barely talk and I was about to collapse from the shaking. This was so so bad.

"Give me five minutes. I had a dress malfunction. I have to fix it."

E.M. GAYLE

"Oh shit!" Trina pushed forward around the stage director bully. "What can I do?"

"Nothing. I can fix it, it's just going to take me a few minutes."

"Okay. Will do. But I'm going to stand right here in case you need my help. I'm not leaving you alone. Casey can tell the FBI to hold their fucking horses."

Any other time I would have laughed to hear Trina lose her unflappable cool. But this was no laughing matter. I closed and relocked the door before dashing back to the dressing table. I pushed everything out of my mind except getting these damned diamonds on this dress. I didn't have the mental bandwidth for anything else. One by one I methodically glued them into place.

All I could do now was hope they all stayed in place and no one questioned them. The official details about the dress that would be released to the public listed two options for the medallion. Ten carats of real diamonds in the form of small chips, or larger Swarovski crystals. The crystals were bigger and thus would lend the dress more sparkle. The exact item now lying on my table. I grabbed the pouch, stuffed them in my pocket and would dispose of them in the first trash can I could find. I wasn't about to try and pass those off as the real thing. It was a miracle Ronin's trick had worked the first time, it wasn't going to happen a second time.

I slipped outside and practically ran into Trina. "Jesus," I said, covering the diamond medallion with my hands to ensure none of them came loose.

"Sorry. I just didn't want to leave you alone. Is everything okay with the dress?" She looked me up and down, eyeing every detail up close.

"Yes. It's fine. But I think we have bigger problems to worry about, right?"

"I don't know." She tipped her head in the direction of several men dressed in black suits and ties who were glaring in our direction. "Casey called Gabe, and he is demanding his lawyer be present before they do anything."

"What exactly are they asking for?"

She lowered her voice to barely a whisper. "They want to search your office." My stomach plummeted and my vision blurred a little. That fucker had set me up. I didn't care how dangerous he was, I was going to kill him.

"Okay, well, we are going to let Gabe handle them for now and we are going to finish this show. Has anyone said anything about that?"

She shook her head. "We're halfway and it's going great."

I waited for the other shoe to drop.

"What? Don't look at me like that. I'm serious. I don't know what the heck is going on back here, but out there, everyone is really happy. I expect presales to start breaking records before the night is over."

I wanted to celebrate this moment so bad, but I was being pulled in so many directions, it was impossible to keep up with them all. "Go then," I urged. "Get the next group of girls out there. You don't need me."

Trina leaned in, her eyes glassy from trying not to cry. "Thank you," she whispered at my ear a moment before she broke away and hustled across to the next line of girls waiting for their turn on the runway. As soon as I could tear my eyes away from the excitement across the room, I tapped out a message to Rock, letting him know what was going on.

Ronin screwed the plan. Homeland Security here to investigate. Find him before he makes another move. Also, dad in audience *with* my sister! Have to help her.

I hit send and closed my messaging app as Gabe descended on me.

CHAPTER 18

Rock

From the moment I kissed Nova goodbye, the world had gone to shit.

Now, I was staring down at a text from the woman in question and left wondering what the hell had gone wrong.

"I've got news." JD slapped down a file folder on the table in front of me.

"Great. I hope it helps because the shit has hit the fan and I've got a lot to unfuck."

"What happened?"

"First yours. I need to think." Before I ended

E.M. GAYLE

up backstage at a fashion show, strangling Ronin fucking Kavanaugh with my bare hands.

"It's good news, and then a fuck-ton of bad news. The good is we don't believe Kavanaugh is actually here to marry your girl. That's likely his cover story, though, since he's actually come to avenge his family. Which also means she might be in more danger than you thought."

"I hope that's not all you have because Ronin just let that shit out of the bag with Nova." I didn't need to tell him the details, especially if he already knew. My anger that Nova had never said a word about a first husband after all our talk about being honest still threatened my control. The last thing I wanted to do was talk about it. "Anything else?"

"You tell me. The story I got is that Kavanaugh's grandfather came to Vegas five years ago to marry a Cullotta and form an alliance with one of the New York families. There was no information on a name for the bride, but the timing coincides perfectly with Nova's eighteenth birthday so it was easy enough to put two and two together. *If* that's what the plan was. The thing that bothers me is the fact Tel was unable to dig up any record of a marriage. Not only was a marriage certificate

FALLEN ANGEL

never filed, there wasn't even an application for one in the first place. We're not sure what to make of that yet, but it doesn't work with the rest of the information we've obtained. To make matters even more complicated, the senior capo from New York has been missing since the night he arrived in Vegas, and the family has been in a near constant state of chaos over it. A lot of infighting as the different branches fought for a new leader."

Surprisingly, the depth of his information did enhance what I heard and made a little more sense out of Nova and Ronin's conversation. I'd need to think on it to see what I could do with it. Right now, I was pissed about Nova not telling me about her past and ready to throttle Ronin for trying to use it against her. But something about all of this nagged at me, and I couldn't quite put my finger on it. The fact my team missed all of this in their investigation? Agency resources sucked ass.

"You don't seem too surprised by any of this."

"Kavanaugh was waiting for Nova in her office. He pretty much revealed his reason for being here. Thanks to the app you had installed on her tablet, I heard every word. Although why that bastard would tell her now makes no sense. I think what-

E.M. GAYLE

ever his plans are he intends to complete them tonight. He's already sicced homeland security on her and she is being served a search warrant now."

"He's creating a diversion."

"Exactly."

"So how do you plan on handling that?"

"Not much I can do for the time being. My hands are legally tied. But we do know that Nova doesn't have those diamonds, so they aren't going to find anything, which means we're going to find that bastard and figure out exactly what he's up to. Then there's Cullotta. He's at the show sitting in the goddamned front row like he's some kind of fucked up proud father. Just waiting to pick her off the moment he can. He also brought her sister. Since she's his leverage against Nova, we need to get to her."

JD's face turned to granite but he nodded. I wasn't telling him anything he didn't already know. Several of the MC guys were already there in the audience, and still others were posing as workers backstage. So far all their bases were covered. So how Ronin had escaped their notice baffled me. He moved like a goddamned ghost.

"Axel can track the girl. Got a picture?"

"Yeah, hang on." I rifled through the case files

on my tablet until I found one and then forwarded it to him.

He yanked out his phone. "That'll work." He tapped out a message and waited. "Okay he's on the move. He'll handle it."

"Let me know. I have to get word to Nova it's taken care of. I'm not letting that fucker get to her."

"Tracker online?" JD asked. "Do we need more eyes on Nova?"

"The tracker is good, and Houston is already en route to take Nova's back. He'll make sure she's covered for whatever bullshit Homeland tries to pull. We need eyes on Kavanaugh. He's the wild card in all this."

"What about Cullotta? I wouldn't underestimate him."

"He's not going anywhere without those diamonds. He'll go after Nova first chance he gets, and we'll be there to intercept, right? She is the priority."

My father grunted. I didn't like the feeling I was getting from him, but it was going to have to work. I started to walk away and get myself in place, when I stopped and turned back. "I'd like you to stick with me."

JD's eyebrows lifted nearly to his hairline. "Planning to be my babysitter?"

"In case you haven't noticed, I don't have the backup of the FBI on this one. Not only have I let myself get personally involved, but I've diverged from protocol at every turn. I'm walking a tightrope out there."

"Lots of moving pieces."

"Exactly. Hence why we stick together. We can work better that way."

The look JD gave me was pure skepticism, with a healthy dose of disbelief. "I get that you want first crack at Cullotta, but if you really want to help me this has to go a different way. It's too dangerous for you or your guys to make a move on Cullotta at the moment. Too many eyes and way too many cellphones to capture you on video. This is a really important event for Nova, so I'd prefer to keep the rest of this investigation discreet, if you get my drift."

He answered with a grunt and I figured that was the best I was going to get. He thought I didn't understand the need for vengeance, but I did. All too well. I'd just chosen a different path than him all those years ago.

"Let's go then." He sounded as about excited as I felt.

I checked my gun one last time to ensure it was fully loaded with the safety in place. I then tucked it into the holster at my side and grabbed my jacket. I didn't bother asking JD if he was carrying.

Of course he was.

CHAPTER 19

Nova

I wiped the sweat from my brow as the final model turned away and headed out onto the stage. The last ten hours had been the most grueling of my life. Between dresses that needed repairs, one of the models getting sick moments before she was due to hit the runway and a dozen other hiccups just like those, I was happy to see the show about to come to an end.

Never mind the Homeland Security agents still working their way somewhat discreetly through all of the backstage rooms in their quest

E.M. GAYLE

to find those wretched diamonds. I cursed the moment I'd decided to steal them from Vincent's plane in the first place.

Worst. Idea. Ever.

Gabe's attorney had failed to thwart the agents from executing their warrant, but he'd convinced someone that the search and seizure either had to wait until the end of the show, or they could look without alarming or interfering.

They'd chosen the latter.

They'd started in my office, and after finding nothing useful, they'd methodically gone room by room. They weren't going to find anything unless someone suddenly realized the crystals on my medallion weren't crystals.

Either way, my nerves were shot. Much more of this and I wouldn't be able to avoid the oncoming nervous breakdown.

"Nova. They're calling for you."

I lifted my head. "What?" Trina was standing just backstage with her clipboard and headset, looking at me with expectation in her eyes.

"Josi is on her last turn, and the crowd is already chanting your name," she said.

"What?" I apparently couldn't string any words together as the adrenaline of the night crashed over me.

FALLEN ANGEL

"Shit. Someone get her some water." Tina rushed over to me, and wrapped her arms around my shoulders. "Take slow, deep breaths. And don't make any sudden moves. I've got some experience with panic attacks, and I'll get you through this and out there before you know it."

"I'm not having a panic attack. At least I don't think so. I've got a hell of a headache, but I'm dealing with it. I'm just overwhelmed. That was a lot of work."

Trina and the other crew, now all standing at my side, smiled. "You bet your ass it was," one of them said.

We all laughed. Everyone on my team deserved a raise, and I would be sure to give them one the minute we recovered from this show.

"What's going on?" Josi joined us. She had been the very first model I ever worked with and I loved her like a sister. Of course, she towered over my five-foot nine frame, but that's why she was the model and I wasn't. Her body could make a paper sack look good.

"Nova's having a panic attack."

"I am NOT having a panic attack. I'm just overly excited about the end of the show. And I'm tired."

E.M. GAYLE

Josi's smiled widened. "Girl, I hear you. We all deserve a hot soak and a bottle of wine tonight. But Nova, you've got to get out there. The crowd is going wild and they want you. Just listen."

We all quieted down and I put all my focus on hearing the noise from the other side of the curtain. It took me a minute, but the chant finally came through.

Nova. Nova. Nova. Nova. Nova.

Tears immediately welled in my eyes, and I fought to keep them back.

Trina sprang forward and gently pressed tissues to the corners. "Don't you dare. You can't ruin your makeup now. You are about to be photographed by every major news outlet and splashed across every internet site you can think of."

She was right. I tipped my head back and blinked several times, taking those deep breaths she had recommended. After a few seconds, the burning at my tear ducts dissipated and I faced forward once again. "What about my hair? Is that still okay?"

"Nova. You could go out there bawling your eyes out and you would still look gorgeous. Your hair is great, the dress is sublime, so just get out there and do your thing. Shine."

FALLEN ANGEL

God, I had the best team. I looked at each one of them as they alternately squeezed my hands and nudged me towards the curtain.

"Break a leg," Josi called.

I laughed. I'd always thought it was such a strange tradition to wish someone that, but I also appreciated the superstition behind it. As always, Trina was in perfect harmony with the show. Just as I was about to reach the curtain, it swooshed open, and I emerged directly onto the runway.

The crowd surged to their feet. Flashbulbs went off, one right after another, as I continued my walk to the end of the stage. At first I could see almost nothing, reminding me what the models went through every time they came out with a new outfit to show off. But after a few minutes, my eyes began to adjust, and I could start to see people as well as the various lights moving around stage to follow my progress. With my smile plastered to my face, I internally counted out the steps as we'd done in rehearsals.

With little experience at this, Josi had given me the rundown on her tips and tricks. People were shouting, but there was simply too much going on for me to make out their comments or questions. That would all have to wait until the press conference scheduled for tomorrow.

I recognized many of the faces as press I had either dealt with or worked with in the past, but the first truly familiar face was that of—Ronin.

He had a great seat right up front and not too far away from the press. Not the seat I had arranged for him. He'd have paid handsomely to upgrade. He smiled at me, and I got the impression of a predatory wolf who gave no fucks about anyone but himself, which seemed fitting.

Shithead.

It took a lot of self-control not to flip him the bird or worse for what he'd done and the position he'd put me in. The minute I was off this stage, he and I were going to have a lot of words.

I turned to face a different direction. I wasn't going to give him any more satisfaction than he was already taking on his own.

Nina and Zia were there, as were their respective men, Gabe and Vincent. They were wildly clapping and shouting at me, and Zia gave me a thumbs up. It thrilled me to see them so happy, but I knew for Gabe, this moment wasn't the celebration he'd been expecting.

I owed him and Nina so much for taking such an expensive gamble on me and my designs, and this mess I had brought to their door was not how I wanted to repay them. My only hope seemed to be in Homeland Security not finding anything worth a further investigation. I had to fight the urge not to cover the diamonds. I had not been thinking about parading them in front of everyone and God when I'd gotten the brilliant idea to glue them to my dress.

The smiles from my friends, however, reminded me that this might be my only chance to enjoy the fact my designs were being applauded by the entire room. Compartmentalizing my fear of being caught, Ronin's motives, and what else my father might have in store for me, I smiled back at them and waved.

I had to have faith that Rock and his family were at my back, like they'd promised.

Did enjoying this moment make me some kind of sociopath?

I hoped not because I'd paid in blood, sweat, and tears to get to this moment and I wasn't giving it up. Fuck Ronin, and fuck those diamonds.

As I continued to the end of the runway, I paused and turned left and right, making sure that the photographers could catch my dress at every angle. While designed for me, it was one of my favorites from the collection and we would release it to the public in the coming months if there was enough interest.

About to turn around and head back to the main stage, I caught the eye of someone even more familiar. And my blood went absolutely frigid. The look my father gave me was cold and hateful enough to turn anyone into stone.

I still couldn't believe this was how he'd chosen to get my attention. Thus far, no one had figured out who I really was, and I desperately wanted to keep it that way. And not for the first time, I was grateful I'd taken the time to legally change my name.

So what the hell was *he* hoping to accomplish with this stunt? He didn't smile when I caught his gaze with mine, and my own pasted-on smile nearly faltered. The last time I'd seen him had not gone well, and he looked no happier to see me now. Ice cold fear prickled my skin like a thousand tiny needles poking me at once. All of Rock's warnings rushed through my brain. If he was right, and my father knew about the diamonds....

My stomach pitched and for a minute I thought I was going to throw up right here on the runway, when I realized I'd missed my cue to turn around. All I had to do was raise my hand to the crowd once more and wave, walk backstage, and this would all be over.

As the event had progressed, more and more security had arrived backstage, and I could only assume that had been Rock's doing. They were waiting for me just fifty yards away.

A few more dozen flashes, I dropped my arm, and walked back to the curtain. It opened when I approached, and I caught sight of one more face from the corner of my eye. Rock.

I almost tripped. Dammit. The myriad of events converging at once made it nearly impossible to focus. This whole darn mess was out of control. All I really wanted to do was smack the smirk from Ronin's face, tell my father and his stupid goon to go fuck themselves, and then let Rock know how I really felt about him and hope like hell that after what he'd overheard, things were not ruined between us. I wanted him always. Overprotective alpha male nonsense included.

First though, I had to face the impossible and talk to my father.

He would take the diamonds and then Rock would swoop in and arrest him. Having blood diamonds in his possession pretty much guaranteed a lifetime prison sentence. Consorting with

E.M. GAYLE

terrorists was a no joke offense according to Rock. I still wasn't convinced prison would be enough to put a stop to him. Anthony Cullotta had a lifetime of experience slithering out of difficult and impossible situations. However, for Rock's sake, I had to try.

I wish I'd thought of that when we'd been together instead of staying focused on how much he'd hurt me. That was the problem in a nutshell, though wasn't it?

A couple of seconds later, the curtain closed behind me and everyone backstage rushed me. Flowers and champagne were handed around as we were all inundated by well-wishers and many congratulations. My heart swelled, but my head ached. I was also having trouble catching my breath.

"Oh my God, Nova. That was amazing." Despite everything, it was hard not to be infected by Trina's excitement. She was right. Against all odds and an enormous amount of roadblocks, we'd done it.

"I could not have done it without you."

"Of course you couldn't," she laughed. "But this show is one hundred percent about you and your gorgeous designs. I hope whatever else is going on, you can put it aside for a few minutes

FALLEN ANGEL

and just absorb the significance of this. You need to savor this. Here maybe this will help." Before I could hug her or tell her how much I loved her, Trina produced a bottle of champagne from behind her back and thrust it towards me.

"You are so right. I need this. But only if you share in this moment with me. In fact..." I turned in the direction of the catering table and yelled at all the girls gathered in the area, still wearing my designs. "Everyone grab some glasses and more champagne. It's time for a toast!"

A series of delighted squeals and shouts of joy erupted throughout the room as the women scurried to grab their supplies and gather around us. Next thing I knew, corks were popped and glasses were filled with the bubbly champagne. But it was the smiles on their faces and the pure joy each and every one emitted from being here that made me lose the fight to the tears threatening to fall.

"You can't cry," Trina handed her glass to the model next to her and dug through her fanny pack for tissues, which she then used to dab at my face. "There are going to be a million more pictures taken tonight, so you can't mess up your makeup now."

She was right and I was grateful she looked

239

E.M. GAYLE

out for me. I owed her in more ways than one. "Thank you," I whispered."

"Okay now?" she asked.

I nodded and all the women crowded around us cheered. When I didn't think they were going to settle down, I made a quieting motion with my hand so I could make a proper toast. "I just wanted to take a moment to thank all of you for being here and for all of your hard work. Without each and every one of you, this night would not have been possible. Creating a show like this is an enormous effort, and well, I owe the success to everyone involved. From the bottom of my heart, thank you so much." I raised my glass higher and toasted every glass I could reach.

I drank deeply, appreciating the quality of the champagne The Sinclair had provided. One of the smartest things I'd done was in getting to know Gabe and Nina. I needed to find them and thank them personally, but the backstage area was more chaotic than when we'd began.

"To Nova," one of the girls in the back yelled and the rest of the women followed suit. Glasses were raised and clinked again, more champagne got consumed and if I squinted my eyes narrow enough and shut out all the extra noise in my

FALLEN ANGEL

head, I could only see the level of success in front of me. And it looked really really good.

"Congratulations, Nova."

Oh God, that voice, just behind me. It reminded me of that night on my balcony when I'd been waiting for him. My nipples tightened, butterflies fluttered in my stomach. I desperately wanted to go back to that night and repeat it all over again. I may not have known his name, but in hindsight I'm glad I didn't. If he had told me who he was before we gotten involved, none of that would have ever happened and I would have missed out on what were the best parts of my life so far.

I turned, taking in the gorgeousness of Rock Reed dressed in his trademark black suit, black shirt and black tie. Standing there with a smirking grin on his face, he looked good enough to eat. Or beg. I wanted to plead with him.

If we left right this minute, maybe we could get far enough away that neither my father or Ronin could create any more trouble for us. The ache in my chest deepened. I wasn't supposed to fall in love in the midst of my life falling apart. But I did.

He must have sensed something in me

E.M. GAYLE

because he stepped forward and gathered me in his arms. "I know this wasn't exactly how you wanted this night to go, but despite everything, it's still clear to everyone here what a gorgeous, talented woman you are."

"I love you," I blurted, my eyes going wide and covering my mouth as soon as the words were out. There was no way that was the right time to say that. I started to say as much when he swooped in and kissed me, his tongue parting my lips and devouring me. I wrapped my arms around his neck and kissed him back with all the desperation and feeling I couldn't hold back. If he wasn't ready to hear the words, I would worry about that later. We still had a lot to talk about.

"Holy shit. That's hot." The women still gathered shrieked and cheered. It was more than a little scandalous for me to be kissing a man not my fiancé at this point, but either these women didn't know or they didn't care. I was past the point of caring. In the grand scheme of things, being with him for even a moment more was more important than my reputation.

"You two really should get a room."

I reluctantly pulled from the kiss, probably looking as stunned as I felt, to find many of the MC gathered around us. They'd traded their

FALLEN ANGEL

jeans and T-shirts for black slacks and black button-down shirts, but they still wore the vests with the patches on them making them look even more badass if that were possible. Was there some kind of badass brotherhood dress code I wasn't aware of? It made me itch with the idea of creating a new men's line for men just like these because if all men dressed like this...

"What's going on, Nova? Did you forget to tell us you made some new friends." Trina had sidled up to me and she was eyeing Axel from head to toe.

I opted to ignore her question. What the hell was I supposed to say anyways? Thankfully, Axel stole that moment to introduce himself to Trina, and the next thing I knew he was being drawn into the group of women as well as many of the others.

"Uhm. Do I need to rescue them?"

Rock eyed me carefully. "Nah. They can handle themselves."

"But what about—?"

"If they're needed, they will be available. Trust me. They may look preoccupied, but I guarantee you each one has complete situational awareness and can respond to anything that comes up suddenly."

I wasn't sure I had that same level of confidence, but I did trust Rock and he seemed to know these men very well. Despite the falling out he'd had with the MC all those years ago, he sure seemed to fall right back in with them like they were family. It was an interesting dynamic I hoped I'd have more time to observe.

"So, what's next?" he asked. "Are you still down with the plan? I know this Homeland Security thing has thrown you for a loop. But since you don't have the diamonds anymore, it's going to be a huge waste of time for them. They'll realize that soon and then they'll move on."

I clenched at his mention of the diamonds. I started to tell him the truth when Nina interrupted. "I guess now I understand why your supposed fiancé left at the end of the show, and why your engagement never made sense. But why the fake fiancé if you and Rock were already a thing?"

Oh shit.

Wait.

"Did you say Ronin left?" Both Rock and I asked.

She nodded. "Yeah, right before the final curtain. I thought maybe he was with those other

FALLEN ANGEL

two men he seemed to follow, but I guess he had a different reason to leave."

Well, hell. Rock and I looked at each other.

Rock leaned in and whispered in my ear. "I've got to go. Stay here, and take care of business. We'll do this another way."

I gave him a slight nod, but my frustration ratcheted another one hundred degrees. He disappeared as quickly as he had appeared, and the men who'd been flirting with the models followed suit, all disappearing instantly in the crowd.

So much for a plan...

CHAPTER 20

Nova

Ten minutes later, I didn't think I could answer another question. I needed some air. I wound my way past the backstage area, ignoring the warnings from Homeland Security for me to not go far, and headed down the hall to the more private offices. I couldn't understand anything. Why would Ronin leave, and who had he been following? My father? If so, what the hell were they up to?

Had I missed something? Or had he gone to kill my—

I heard a muffled shout from down the hall.

E.M. GAYLE

Not knowing what to do next, I cursed the fact I didn't have my phone or my tablet having left both behind before I went down the runway. Screw it. I ran in the direction of the noise. If nothing else, I still had the diamonds my father wanted and maybe they would save me after all. Or buy me some time before Rock found me.

The shouting had stopped, but I could still hear someone the faint sounds of someone talking. I pressed my ear to one door after another until I found one that seemed like I would be it. On a deep breath and a prayer, I pushed it open and did my best to see without being seen.

Dammit. I could not stop walking into trouble.

"Not the best timing, Nova, dear." Ronin spoke to me without taking his eyes or his gun off my father. "Why aren't you at the show?"

"Because I figured out you set me up. Show or no show. Enough is enough. I'm tired of playing games with you both, and it's time to end this once and for all. What do you want? Tell me what I can do to end this?"

"That's fair enough. Since you're here, I can break it to you now that I'm not going to marry you. Although if it makes you feel better, I did seriously consider it. Watching you have sex with

FALLEN ANGEL

Agent Reed was one of the highlights of this trip. In another time and place, I believe the two of us could have had some fun together."

"What the fuck?" My father cut in, turning to look at me. "You're disgusting. I don't know how you turned into such a little whore. That is not how we raised you."

"That's because I raised myself. I might have lived in a house that you paid for, but that's about the extent of what you did. Even mother couldn't be bothered with me. You both treated me like dirt on your shoe."

"Ungrateful little bitch," he rasped, his face an angry shade of red.

"Hey." Ronin waved his gun back and forth to get Anthony's attention. "How dare you talk to your daughter that way. What the hell is wrong with you? Jesus. This is exactly why someone like me is here right now. You don't deserve to breathe her air, let alone speak to her."

"Screw you. You think you know what happened that night. But you don't. She is not the innocent you seem to think she is."

My blood froze at my father's words. His lack of honor shocked me even now, after everything. He was about to throw me under the bus to save himself.

"He's right," I admitted. "I didn't know that man was your grandfather. Not that it would have made a difference back then. I was young and scared and hurt." Tears I desperately didn't want to shed burned behind my eyes at the memories. "I didn't know what else to do."

"See. She is the one who killed him. She betrayed your family *and* mine."

Ronin seemed to ponder this information, while looking as unsurprised as ever. Once again, I got the feeling he was several steps ahead of all of us.

"So you are innocent?" he asked, looking at Anthony. "You had nothing to do with his death? The plan to lure him to Vegas with the promise of a marriage to an unwilling virgin wasn't your idea at all?"

I blinked, not sure I was comprehending what he was getting at.

"Of course not. Arnald and I had a business arrangement plain and simple. We were going to create one of the greatest alliances this country has ever seen. Together, our families would have ruled this country."

Ronin barked out a laugh. "My grandfather was a sick old bastard. He usually preferred his women even younger than eighteen. The only

FALLEN ANGEL

way she would have interested him is if you promised him something more. And we both know it wasn't some bullshit alliance. Our organization was on the verge of crushing yours. We were days away from a complete takeover of your organization and she was your Hail Mary."

My mouth dropped open at this new information. What the hell was happening?

"That's ridiculous."

"Is it? His disappearance threw our family into chaos, and it took us years to recover. In the meantime, with us out of the way, your business flourished. You stole deals that were ours, attempted alliances with our allies, and kept us in turmoil. We couldn't even retaliate because no one knew for sure what happened and no one dared risk a war with an outside family when we had an internal fight to deal with."

My father was shaking his head, while mine was exploding. I should have kept my mouth closed, but I couldn't think straight. "But he didn't kill, Mr. Onofrio. I did. My memories may be hazy, but I do still remember."

Ronin turned to me again. "Have you ever wondered why your memories of that night are so murky? Or why your father sprung that

E.M. GAYLE

marriage on you with no warning or preparation whatsoever?"

I shook my head, utterly speechless. I definitely didn't understand.

"He set you up. You were nothing more than a pawn, in case his plan backfired. He had you drugged, faked a wedding ceremony, and then invited my grandfather to rape you."

"That's not—"

"It is, and your man Luca turned on you like the rat you both are. I got every last juicy detail out of him before he choked on his own blood. Although he did give me this nice gun with his fingerprints all over it after he tried to shoot me."

My hand flew up and covered my mouth to contain my cry. Not because I had any love lost for Luca, but because it was all beginning to ring too true. The celebratory drink my mother had given me just before I went to my father's office, the rushed ceremony, the forced consummation, it all fell heinously into place.

"You motherfucker!" I reached for my father, but Ronin grabbed my hands and swiftly twisted them and locked them behind my back while pulling me against his back.

"Nope. We can't have that. Not that you don't deserve your revenge, but this one is mine."

"What do you want?"

"There is nothing you could give me that would change the outcome. You, Anthony Cullotta, have betrayed your family, my family and have threatened to ruin our business. You are a disgusting pig of a man, who deserves much worse than a bullet to the brain. But I've grown tired of this game, and it's time to move on."

"No, I—please."

The sound of a muffled gunshot filled my ears and there was suddenly a hole in my father's forehead. His mouth was still open and his eyes stared my way for a moment before he crumpled to the ground. A cold wave of sorrow washed over me as I stood in horror and watched blood ooze from his wound. My father was dead just like that.

"They always beg. It's disgusting."

Before I could recover my wits or figure out what he was talking about, Ronin released my hands and pushed me gently to the other side of the room. "I can't really say I'm sorry you had to see that, but it wasn't my intent. Like I said. Bad timing, babe."

"What happens now? Are you going to kill me too?" I was too numb for the fear to sink in. But

E.M. GAYLE

it seemed rather logical. I was now a witness to murder. He was never going to let me go.

"I don't think that's necessary, do you? Even if you tell the Boy Scout I did it, the evidence tells a different story, and you've got as much motive as I do. I think he's too far gone for you to risk you ending up in jail."

I wasn't sure what to think. "You set up Luca for this? Is he still alive?"

Ronin shrugged and I didn't know how to take that. I might also be better off if I didn't have any more details. I didn't want to lie any more than I had to. "I figure you got the short end of the straw with that one as your father. He's had that coming for a long time, and you're better off without him.

I nodded. I was still reeling at how far he'd gone to hurt me, even as I continued to stare at his lifeless body on the floor.

"The way I look at it, I did you a favor. There's going to be a power struggle your eldest brother is going to have to face, but let's hope he's less of a dick than your father. Otherwise, I'll be right back out here doing this shit again."

"I doubt that's going to be necessary. My brother is a bit of a jerk, but he's a lot smarter than him."

FALLEN ANGEL

"Look at me, Nova." I slowly tore my gaze from the body on the floor and turned to look at Ronin. "You owe me now. You wanted your freedom and now you have it."

"But this isn't what—"

"It's done. Go back to lover-boy, and enjoy your life. But one day, I will be back and need something from you, no questions asked. Those are my terms, take them or leave them."

Fuck. I was so tired of making deals. But what choice did I have? "Fine, but—"

"No buts. One favor. That's the deal."

I nodded. He wasn't going to give me any other choice. As he stepped around me to leave, he stopped and turned back, pointing at my stomach. "And I'd dump those diamonds while you can. You don't want to get caught by Homeland Security with those.

I grabbed at the medallion still at my waist. "How did you know?"

He smirked. "I'm not stupid, babe. Don't pretend you are either."

"Why the hell did you put those diamonds in my office and call Homeland Security in the first place? I nearly got caught red-handed thanks to you."

He shrugged. "I needed a diversion, and it was

E.M. GAYLE

the easiest to create. I figured lover-boy would swoop in and save you. Glad to see you saved yourself."

I absolutely should not have felt a puff of pride at his praise. The jerk had just killed my father in front of me. I shuddered to think of the amount of therapy it would take to forget all of this.

"You seriously do not deserve any favors," I snarled at him. "How the hell am I going to explain all of this to Rock?"

He lifted his shoulders again and smiled as he disappeared through the door. "See you in the future, Nova."

I looked down at the medallion on my dress to see a splatter of blood covering a few of the diamonds. My stomach churned and a gag clenched my throat. I had to get out of here, but he was right about these. I finagled my fingers underneath the medal and struggled with the clasp holding it to the material. I couldn't quite get a hold of the clasp so that I could turn the lever loose.

I was trying not to panic, but every second that ticked by, I expected someone to burst through the door and catch me with my father's dead body. As my fingers continued to refuse to work properly, a scream surged in my chest.

Frustrated and desperate, I tried to rip it free, but it wouldn't come loose. Oh. My. God.

"This is ridiculous."

I forced myself to stop fighting it and take a breath before trying it again. Moving slowly this time, I slid my finger behind the medallion, felt for the clasp and gently rolled it to free the pin, nearly screaming in relief when it slid open.

However, before I could make another move the door opened and Rock walked in. His gaze immediately registered Anthony on the floor and then he locked on me. "Jesus Christ, Nova. Are you all right?"

"What the fuck?" JD roared from behind him, and he wasn't alone. One second I was alone and the next the entire club had filled the small conference room.

"Nova." Rock rushed to my side and cupped my face with both hands. Just seeing him here, feeling the safety of his hands on me nearly made me collapse.

"I'm fine. I'm not hurt." My lip trembled as I tried to hold it together.

"What the hell happened?" That question

came from more than one of the men at the same time.

What was I supposed to say? If I told Rock that Ronin did this, I could be his next target for ratting him out. But if I lied to Rock again. Even I couldn't live with that anymore.

"Ronin," he said, answering his own question.

I bit my lip and held my silence, which meant we both knew he'd guessed right.

"That motherfucker," JD looked particularly angry as he stared down at the body. "A bullet to the brain. What bullshit. That bastard deserved far worse."

"Dad!"

Everyone in the room turned to look at Rock. That was the first time I'd heard him use that word, and judging by the looks on all of their faces, they weren't used to it either.

JD turned to his son, his face hard. "Don't start." Then he turned to me. "I'm sorry, Nova. I'm not trying to upset you, but that man—" He didn't finish his thought, but the jerk of muscle in his jaw and the dark look in his eyes was more than enough.

"I'm not upset. At least not in the way I think I should be. His capacity for evil was so much worse than even I knew."

A chill worked up my arms as I thought of everything Ronin had said. Every word sounded like it was from a horror movie script, not real life. I rubbed my arms.

"We need to get her out of here so we can deal with this." JD waved in the direction of my father's body. I was too afraid to look down. I never wanted to see anything like that again.

"Did you touch anything?"

I shook my head.

"What about the gun?"

"Ronin said it belonged to Franciso, my father's right-hand man. I don't know what happened to him, and I'm pretty sure I don't want to know."

"Smart," Axel said, coming forward to crouch down and inspect the weapon without touching it. "I'd have to check to be sure, but I'd bet it was fired at least twice today."

"No. He only shot my father once. In the—the head."

"We don't have to talk about it now. Let's get you out of here and backstage where you're supposed to be."

I nodded, trying to pull my thoughts together to get out of here. I took a slow, deep breath and

E.M. GAYLE

tried to slow my racing heartbeat. "Let's go now. I need to get out of here."

"Sure thing." He hesitated and looked over at JD and Axel.

"We got this. Get your girl out of here and I'll contact you after."

Rock nodded, reaching for my hand. When I tried to grab hold, I realized I still had the medallion clutched in my palm.

"Oh my God. I almost forget. I have the diamonds!" I held up my hand and showed him the gold piece I'd removed from my dress.

"Excuse me?" He asked, looking at me like I'd lost my mind.

"The diamonds. Ronin set me up and planted them in my dressing room. By sheer luck I was in there trying to send you a message when I found them. I panicked and didn't know what to do. I had to get them out of there, so I hot-glued them to this. I've been wearing them for hours and pretty much freaking out the whole time."

"You hot glued millions of diamonds to your dress?" Rock's question caused several of the men to snicker.

"Sounds pretty ingenious to me. Maybe smuggling via fashion will become the next thing."

Both Rock and I shot JD a look. "That's not even funny," I said.

"All you have to do is just pull them off. Hot glue holds really well, but it's also easy to remove." I plucked off each gem and dropped them one by one into his outstretched hand.

"He stared at them for a few seconds before he handed them to JD. Clean them up and leave them on the body. If these are recovered, no one's going to care too much about a dead mafia don. Let's just hope they're real this time."

"No. You don't think he would pull that again, do you?"

"With Ronin, there is no telling. He is obsessed with games. I guarantee he didn't walk out of here without a plan for how to keep it going later."

A twinge of guilt constricted my chest. I was not going to open that can of worms today. Maybe never. The last thing I needed was Rock and Ronin in a never-ending cat and mouse situation. They were both relentless, and Rock would never let Ronin hold a favor over my head.

"How did you find me anyways?" I was stupid and left my tablet behind.

E.M. GAYLE

Tel held up his tablet. "Tracker in your necklace."

"You never take that necklace off, so we attached a micro device to it just in case." Rock explained.

I looked at him, unsure what to say. "Thanks, I guess."

"I told you I wasn't taking chances and I meant it. I'm just sorry we didn't get here sooner. Next time I see Ronin I'm going to kick his ass for this stunt and then haul his ass to jail."

I couldn't blame him for feeling that way. I was officially overspending any more time with my former pseudo fiancé.

"Can we go now?" I couldn't take another minute in this room. I wasn't going to breathe easy until I started putting this behind me.

Plus, I couldn't shake the feeling that we all needed to get as far away from this scene as possible. I had a lot to process, and that wasn't going to be easy if Homeland Security caught us standing over a dead body with the diamonds nearby.

CHAPTER 21

Rock

We'd barely cleared the threshold of Nova's destroyed office when I swung her around to face me. "Okay, we're alone. Tell me what in the hell is going on. What did Ronin say to you?"

"The last five years of my life have been a lie. I know I should have told you that I'd been married before, but I—how was I supposed to tell you that I killed someone?" She blurted. I don't know what I expected her to say, but that wasn't it.

"Whoa. Back up. I was talking about Ronin

and your father. You kinda killed someone? How do you kind of do that?"

"I don't know." She plopped down on a chair and proceeded to push her head between her knees. Clearly, she was in shock and needed some time to get her thoughts together. But there was too much at stake and I had to know exactly what happened.

"Tell me," I insisted.

Her head dipped again as if she didn't want to look me in the eyes. "I was eighteen. All I remember is a wedding ceremony my father forced me into. Only I didn't—don't—remember a single detail beyond the wedding ceremony and the sick dread I felt after as I was prepared for my husband. I woke up with blood everywhere and my husband with a knife in his chest. I thought my memory blank was because of the trauma and the fact I didn't want to remember. "

My head reeled as information poured out of her in no discernible order. "Nova." I pushed all of my fingers into my hair and then scrubbed them down my face.

"I know. It's crazy. Hence why I blocked it out of my mind. Or so I thought. Apparently, my memories of that night were all messed up because my father had me drugged."

If Cullotta wasn't already dead, I would have killed him myself.

"I don't know what he gave me, but his intent was clear. He wanted to make me more malleable so I wouldn't fight him on the supposed marriage. But it was all a ruse. He lured Ronin's grandfather there under the guise of marrying me, but it was nothing more than an elaborate plan to kill him and pin it on me."

"God damn." I'd hunted a lot of mafia men in my days, but this was— "He's lucky he's dead. My father was right. A bullet to the head wasn't enough."

She blinked up at me, her eyes glassy with unshed tears and I wanted to kick myself. I needed to keep comments like that to myself. No matter how much hatred ran through her veins right now, she'd still witnessed a man she once loved be murdered. I crouched down beside her and cupped her cheek before gently pulling her into my arms. "I'm so sorry, Nova. I'm not helping by saying things like that, but hearing this—" I hesitated, reaching for something not so vicious to say. "Someone hurting you tears my heart out. It makes me need to lash out."

"I love you Rock Reed." She pressed her lips to mine and I took that beautiful, sweet kiss and

E.M. GAYLE

devoured her mouth. I couldn't express how devastated I was by what she went through, but I could find a way to let her know how much she meant to me.

She clung to me and I clung right back. "I am never letting you—" I didn't even get to finish my thought before there was a stern knock at the door. "Dammit. What now?"

"You okay, Nova?" She still looked shell shocked and I wanted to get one of her friends in here to sit with her while I started sorting shit out. But first we had to go over a few unpleasant things. There were going to be questions sooner rather than later.

"If anyone asks you anything about your father, Ronin, or those diamonds, you know nothing. Got it? If someone starts interrogating you, you ask for a lawyer and call Gabe for help. His lawyers are fucking sharks. Do exactly what they tell you to."

"Do I need a lawyer?" she whispered, her voice shaking.

He sure as hell hoped not. "I'm telling you just in case. You can't be too careful when it comes to the letter of the law, and trust me if there is any question at all, you want a lawyer. Okay?" She nodded, but I still wasn't sure she was in the right frame of mind for this.

I'd called in some favors, and hopefully my contacts would arrive shortly and put this mess into the correct perspective. However, there were no guarantees since I couldn't one hundred percent control the information getting out. Hence, I wanted a goddamn lawyer in here to protect her as well.

I crossed to the door and discovered two of the Homeland Security agents waiting on the other side. They'd been searching for hours and were bound to start asking questions. And since this was the absolute worst timing possible, they were here.

"We're looking for Ms. Cullotta."

Shit.

I didn't have to turn and see her face to know that Nova was about to start freaking out now that they'd identified her as Anthony Cullotta's daughter.

"She's here, but I'd like to see badges first before she speaks to you. As well as locate her employer and his attorney to supervise. This is Sinclair property and she is one of their employees."

One of the men narrowed his eyes. "And you

E.M. GAYLE

are?"

"Agent Rock Reed, FBI. I'm reaching for my badge now."

"Same," he said.

I pulled my identification from my breast pocket and traded with them. Then grabbed my cellphone and took two quick pictures so I could send them to my boss. There was nothing wrong with verifying that all of this was on the up and up and maybe I could gain a little insight into what the end goal here was.

"Are you currently conducting an investigation in The Sinclair?"

That was a damned tricky question. Officially I was on leave. Luckily, I had the best cover of all, and I could answer without really answering. "Nova, Ms. Cullotta, is my girlfriend. I am here to attend her show and accompany her to the after party."

"Oh shit," Nova swore behind him. Guess she'd forgotten about the party.

"Can we come in? This shouldn't take long."

I smirked. Famous last words. I stepped back, allowing them access. "Considering you've already destroyed my girlfriend's office in your wasted search, I'm not sure what else she can do for you."

"We just have a few questions."

"Are you acquainted with—" the agent made a show of looking down at his notepad as if he hadn't already memorized every word of every question he intended to ask. "Ronin Kavanaugh?"

"Yes. He's the man my father has arranged for me to marry despite my objections."

I ground my teeth to keep my mouth closed. I should have emphasized the need for only yes or no answers. That kind of detail only opens her up to even more questions they might not have thought of.

"But Agent Reed here is your boyfriend?"

She looked up at me and a slight smile crossed her face. "Yes, we've been dating for several weeks now."

Both agents scribbled notes. Assholes.

"Do you know where Mr. Kavanaugh is now?"

"No."

Much better. He hoped like hell they were wrapping this up soon.

"And your father. Have you seen him today?"

She nodded. "Of course. He was in the audience during the show."

"What about after?"

"Not yet. Although I am sure I will hear from

E.M. GAYLE

him soon, since I informed Mr. Kavanaugh earlier today that I would not be marrying him."

The questions continued, but I started to tune them out. Nova had pulled herself together and was handling herself like a true media star. Considering her experience with the press, I should have known she could deal with two Homeland agents. First, I texted Houston and informed him of what was going on and asked if Gabe and Nina could give Nova an assist. He texted back they were all on their way, including the lawyer.

Good. He'd shut this down immediately and we could get on with working through the other problems.

The next text went to JD, which went unanswered. I couldn't say much over the phone, but he'd know I wanted to talk to him. There were so many balls in the air right now, I didn't know which one to catch first.

There was going to be a shit ton of fallout over Cullotta's death. He may have been a shitty leader, but he'd been the head of a small family that would leave a power vacuum in Vegas. Which meant more problems for law enforcement and criminals alike. It was time to get JD and the club out of Vegas. They might be family, but their visit had bad timing written all over it.

I scrubbed my hand over my face again. Maybe it was time for me to leave the agency. It was impossible for me to see the world in only black and white. I wasn't about to rejoin the club and do the things they did, but I was tired of having my hands tied in ways that meant I had to compromise myself at every turn. Leaving now might leave a cloud of suspicion behind, but I didn't make decisions based on what other people thought.

My phone dinged with an incoming text. I looked down to read it.

JD: We're all clear. Come home and visit soon. Bring the girl.

That was my father. He said so much with so few words, and he apparently liked Nova and I together. That didn't surprise me. She was one hell of a woman.

I shoved my phone back in my pocket without answering. A visit home might be a bit of a minefield of emotions, but it might be nice to let Nova see where exactly I'd come from. No family was perfect, but they all had their moments, and after tonight, we earned a vacation.

A few minutes later, Houston, Gabe, and Nina arrived, followed shortly by the lawyer. As I expected, he made short work of getting rid of the Homeland agents. They were likely to call everyone back in once I reported the body, but until then Nova could breathe easy with her friends at her back.

"What's next?" Houston asked as they both watched Nina and Gabe each offer Nina a hug.

"Is that position in your firm you keep trying to get me to take still open?"

Houston's head snapped sideways so fast it made me laugh. That look of surprise on his face was damned priceless. We'd been taking it slow in getting to know each other again after a decade apart, but it was time to finally put that to rest for good.

"Are you serious?"

I lifted my shoulders, since I was feeling him out, not making a commitment. "Keeping my options open is all."

"Just say the word, brother. I've been waiting." His answer felt good *and* right.

After the agents were gone, I sat next to Nova, grabbed her hand, and filled everyone in on what was about to happen. Definitely not protocol, but it was a little late for that at this point.

"We need to brace ourselves for what's going to come next. You may have gotten rid of Homeland, but things are about to get a whole lot worse before they get better. Since the after party is set to take place in Zia's Kitchen, I would suggest everyone head there now. Stay there. I'm going to control the fallout as best I can, but Gabe,"—I looked over at the hotel manager —"you are going to have to control the press. Whatever connections and influence you have, use them. I can certainly keep my part out of the news, and I suggest you all do the same."

"What are you talking about?" Gabe asked, his confusion evident.

I took a deep breath, squeezed Nova's hand, and dropped the bomb about Cullotta's murder. I'm pretty sure Gabe's face turned about fifty shades of red as the implications of a murdered crime boss on his hotel property sank in.

"I know you have a million questions, but there's no time to answer them. You'll probably have about an hour or so to coordinate how the coroner will get in and get out without being seen by the press, so I suggest you don't waste any time."

E.M. GAYLE

"Fuck." His grated curse was the exact sentiment for how they all felt right now.

His lawyer touched his arm and whispered something to him that I couldn't make out. Probably for the best I didn't hear whatever plans they made.

"Where?"

"Small conference room in the back of the convention area behind the auditorium."

"Dammit," he cursed. "There are still a shit ton of people out there."

"Then I suggest you get to work."

While Gabe looked ready to explode, he wasted no time. He pulled his wife to the side and spoke to her and then he, Houston and the attorney left.

"What about us?" Nina asked. "We're just supposed to party like nothing happened?"

"It's what everyone expects. The Sinclair has just co-hosted their first successful fashion show, and the press and guests are going to expect a big blowout. So give it to them and keep them too busy for anything else." I brought Nova's hand to my mouth and kissed her fingers. "It's what she deserves."

"I'm so sorr—"

Nina held up her hand to stop Nova from continuing. "Don't you dare apologize. This is not your fault." I doubted Nova believed that, but she nodded and the two women embraced.

When they pulled away, Nina gasped. "Oh no! Your dress. What happened?"

To her credit, Nova didn't blink or hesitate. "The medallion got damaged. But don't worry. This is exactly why I created duplicates of everything." She crossed to her closet and unwrapped a second identical dress to the one she had on right down to the fancy jeweled piece that seemed like it held the dress together, but actually didn't.

"You are such a clever girl."

Nova laughed. "Paranoid more like. However, I'll take clever." She smiled with Nina, and while I am sure a part of her was still happy about the success of the show, that smile didn't quite light up her eyes like it normally would. She was going to need some time to absorb and recover from tonight's nightmare.

"Okay, get out, then." Nina pointed to me. "Go do whatever you have to do to make this right. We have a party to get to."

I was torn about leaving her, but I also knew

that she was the strongest woman I had ever met. She could handle this without me hovering over her and growling at the press when they acted like assholes.

"I'll be back as soon as I can. In the meantime, don't answer any questions from anyone about your father without a lawyer present, okay?

"Don't worry, Agent Reed. She's in good hands," Nina reassured me.

Somehow I didn't doubt that. I had not always gotten along with Gabe and his wife, but they did take good care of their own and they considered Nova theirs.

The next twenty-four hours were going to suck, but with a little luck and a whole lot of work, they were all going to be better off at the other end.

When Nina turned back around and began pulling out the alternate dress, I stared deep into Nova's eyes and mouthed *I love you*.

I love you too.

I hoped she was ready for what came next and I sure as hell didn't mean the bullshit we were going to go through tonight. No. Falling in love had not been on my radar, but now that it was, I intended to make her mine in every way imaginable.

EPILOGUE

Rock

Two months later

"Wow. That's great news. I am so happy for you." Nova gripped the phone tighter, her smile a mile wide. Apparently, whatever drama was still going on around her sister had turned out good. The smile she wore was enough to make my chest ache. The last month or two had been the best and the worst.

E.M. GAYLE

Despite everything that had gone down during the fashion show, it had been declared by the press and the industry a wild success. Gabe had done his part and managed to keep the fact Anthony Cullotta had been murdered in his hotel a secret. And since Cullotta's right hand man Luca was the top suspect in the crime since his gun and fingerprints were conveniently found at the scene and then he was subsequently gunned down less than a week later. The FBI had closed the case.

They weren't done with the blood diamonds though. Although them being recovered from Cullotta had made my boss very happy. The investigation, however, would likely never end. They still wanted Romeo Rossi. Despite being deported, he still had a heavy influence in Las Vegas and the agency wasn't going to let it go.

I did, though. Ten plus years of mob hunting under the constraints of the FBI had been enough. Now, if I needed to get my hands a little dirty, no one was around to watch my every move and my results weren't as dependent on whether the evidence could be used in court. I'd still take down bad guys and protect the inno-cent, but life had gotten a whole lot easier, not to mention lucrative. Private investigation and security services paid extremely well and came with all the high-tech toys.

"I'll call you when we get back in town and we can set up a brunch or something. I definitely want to see you before you leave for college."

While the conversation sounded promising, my focus had stayed firmly on my woman. The short halter dress with the flirty lacy ruffle at the bottom that she'd chosen to wear to an MC party was going to get her a shit load of attention.

" That was Carina. My brothers have all agreed that she needs to go to college. They also managed to break the marriage contract my father had signed for her... Why are you looking at me like that?" she asked as she stuffed her phone into her purse.

"I'm wondering why you want me to get into a fight tonight. Or multiple fights more likely."

She wrinkled her brow and frowned. "What are you talking about? What fight?"

"The fights I'm going to have to start with certain club members who are going to be assholes over you in that dress."

The look she gave me might have shut down any other man, but I wasn't any other man. "That's ridiculous. This isn't that sexy. In fact, I went out of my way to choose something that wasn't too tight *or* too short. This is your family, and I'd like their second impression of me to be less anxiety riddled mafia trash and more sassy and classy worthy of your time." She tilted her head and let her hair fall around her shoulders. "And maybe a little hot too."

"You're more than a little hot, Nova. Look at my dick."

Her gaze traveled to my crotch and after her eyes widened at the tenting of my slacks, she bit back a smile.

"I could take care of that for you."

I barely hid the groan from the image of her on her knees taking me down her throat that had popped into my mind. Fuck.

"You'll be lucky if you don't end up over my knee with your legs bound and your panties down, taking my hand to your ass, Sweetheart."

A slow smile spread across her face and I had a feeling about what she would say next.

"I'm not wearing any panties."

Five little words. That's all it took for her to unravel me. "You shouldn't have said that," I warned, my need for control snapping into place.

There were times she liked to push my buttons, and apparently this was going to be one of them.

"I'm sorry, Sir."

I scoffed. As contrite as she sounded, we both knew she wasn't sorry.

"Show me," I ordered, looking down at my phone in my peripheral vision. We weren't late for the party yet, but there was a good chance we would be if I didn't make this quick.

She dropped her purse at her feet, and proceeded to lift the short skirt of her dress. When her bare mound came into view, it took a fair amount of effort to keep my face passive while I swallowed thickly. She was so fucking beautiful, my chest ached.

"Were you planning to go to the party like this?"

She bit her lip. "Not necessarily. I just hadn't gotten around to putting my panties on yet."

In other words, she needed this.

I closed the short distance between us with a savage groan. I don't know what she'd been banking on, but I hoped she was ready for what she got.

I grabbed her face with both hands and dragged her closer, crashing my lips to hers. I had to admit the tension of waiting all day to go to this party had left me on edge. If my sweet angel wanted to be the sacrificial lamb to ease some of it, I would accept.

I dove into that kiss as she eagerly opened under my onslaught. Red hot lust exploded through my veins as the heat between us took over. To her credit, she gave as good as she got, kissing me back with an intensity that rivaled my own.

Shifting one hand to her hair, I fisted the long locks and tipped her face back, plunging us both into the depths of a kiss that would ruin us if we weren't already in love.

Her hands grabbed at my shirt, pulling it up until her fingers hit skin. She curled her long fingernails into my back and raked them down to my waist.

I groaned into her mouth, wanting more, needing her to take so much more. I fisted my hand and pulled us free from the kiss.

"This is going to be quick," I warned a second before walking her backwards to the hotel room desk. There I lifted her on top and without a word of encouragement she tore into the button and zipper of my jeans.

"We have to hurry. Houston and Izzy are going to be knocking on our door any second."

Fuck. "They'll wait. Get my cock out now."

FALLEN ANGEL

I reached between her legs to test her readiness and nearly lost my mind when I found her drenched. "Jesus Christ, woman. Are you trying to kill me?"

"I can't help it. All that grumbling and growling you've been doing today turned me on."

"So glad I could be of service to *you*," I said through gritted teeth as I clenched against the first touch of her hand to my cock when she wrapped her fingers around me.

"I love it when you're grumpy. It's sexy as hell." My eyes rolled to the back of my head because it felt like she was punctuating each of her words with a tight stroke of her hand.

"Fuck, Nova."

"I bet grumpy tastes good. I'd love to find out."

"Next time," I ground out, losing a little more of my control. "When we have time."

Unable to wait a second longer, I reached between us and pushed her hand out of the way. "Wrap your arms around my neck, angel and hang on."

I lined my cock up with her soaked pussy and slid through her slick folds and across the top of her clit.

"Oh yes." He head fell back. "Just like that."

I repeated that move several more times until she could barely breathe, let alone talk. Now that was more like it. "Ms. Sassy Pants done being sassy?"

"Yes, she cried, her legs tightening around my thighs.

Satisfied she was as close as me, I thrusted forward, claiming her, and giving her everything I had in return. I couldn't get over how much having her in my life had changed everything for the better.

I loved her more than I thought possible and now she was all—"Mine!"

"Yes, yes, yes," she screamed as the first squeeze of her orgasm clamped down on my cock.

"Mine," I repeated on the next hard thrust, moving her a few inches along the smooth wood of the desk.

"Harder," she begged and I complied, rattling everything from the surface as I planted myself to the root once again.

"Look at me," I demanded. "Always look at me when I make you come." I barely got the words out and her eyes snapped to mine before the heat of my own release burned up my spine and pulsed into her. I thrusted one last time before crashing our lips together in one final kiss.

By the time we both came down from the high of pleasure, I realized someone was knocking at our door.

"Shit."

She laughed. "I thought you said they could wait?"

I seriously could not get over how lucky I was to have this woman in my life. I leaned forward and kissed her hard. "I can't get enough of you."

"Good thing, because I think you're stuck with me."

"I'm not stuck, Nova. I'm in love. There's a huge difference."

Her eyes glazed over with a sheen of tears. "You're going to make me cry and ruin my makeup and then what will everyone at the party think?"

I threw my head back and roared with laughter. "Babe, your makeup is the least of your worries. No one cares about that. And if they did then they are going to be patting my ass on the back for a job well done. Because you've got the look of a woman who just got fucked."

"Oh my God. Let me down so I can get

cleaned up. And for God's sake answer the door so they will stop."

Reluctantly, I shifted our bodies apart as I shook from laughter. When she tried to bolt to the bathroom, I caught her around the waist and kissed the back of her neck.

"Mine forever," I whispered against her skin.

She shuddered against me and whispered back,

"Forever."

* * *

THANKS SO MUCH FOR READING. I hope you enjoyed the Broken Saint Duet as much as I enjoyed writing it.

WANT to know what's coming next? Or read some upcoming bonus epilogues? Join my newsletter at https://emgayle.com/newsletter

WHO's story do you think should be next? Write to me at eliza@emgayle.com and let me know. You never know what could happen!

. . .

A LOT of characters that were featured in the Broken Saint Duet already have their own stories and you may have missed them.

HOUSTON AND IZZY from the Outlaw Justice Trilogy (also features JD and Axel and the rest of the Sins of Wrath MC)

VINCENT AND ZIA from the Dirty Sins Duet.

ALEX AND HARPER from the Merciless Sinner Duet

GABE AND NINA from Gabe's Obsession and Gabe's Reckoning

ALSO BY E.M. GAYLE

CONTEMPORARY ROMANCE

Mafia Mayhem Duet Series:

MERCILESS SINNER

SINNER TAKES ALL

DIRTY LITTLE SINS

DIRTY BIG SINS

BROKEN SAINT

FALLEN ANGEL

Outlaw Justice Series:

SAVAGE PROTECTOR

RECKLESS PAWN

RUTHLESS REDEMPTION

Purgatory Masters Series:

TUCKER'S FALL

LEVI'S ULTIMATUM

MASON'S RULE

GABE'S OBSESSION

GABE'S RECKONING

Purgatory Club:

ROPED

WATCH ME

TEASED

BURN

BOTTOMS UP

HOLD ME CLOSE

Pleasure Playground Series:

PLAY WITH ME

POWER PLAY

Single Title:

TAMING BEAUTY

WICKED CHRISTMAS EVE

BOOKS WRITING AS ELIZA GAYLE

Southern Shifters Series:

DIRTY SEXY FURRY

MATE NIGHT

ALPHA KNOWS BEST

BAD KITTY

BE WERE

SHIFTIN' DIRTY

BEAR NAKED TRUTH

ALPHA BEAST

ONE CRAZY WOLF

Enigma Shifters:

DRAGON MATED

WOLF BAITED

BEARLY DATED

Devils Point Wolves:

WILD

WICKED

WANTED

FERAL

FIERCE

FURY

Bound by Magick Series:

UNTAMED MAGICK

MAGICK IGNITED

FORCE OF MAGICK

MAGICK PROVOKED

Single titles:

VAMPIRE AWAKENING

WITCH AND WERE

Made in the USA
Middletown, DE
01 September 2021